The Viking

Crap

Not Historical

cliché ridden

By

Marti Talbott

*

At not quite fifteen, Stefan's father finally let him board the longship Sja Vinna to take part in his first Viking raid. Yet, the battle was not at all what he expected and he soon found himself alone and stranded in Scotland.

Thirteen-year-old Kannak's problem was just as grave. Her father deserted them and the only way to survive, she decided, was to take a husband over her mother‘s objections. Suddenly she was helping a hated Viking escape. Could Kannak successfully hide a Viking in the middle of a Scottish Clan? And why was someone plotting to kill the clan's beloved laird?

This book is suitable for ages 14 and above.

CHAPTER 1

It was near the end of Stefan Rossetti's fourteenth year that his father, the commander of the Viking longship *Sja Vinna* and its fleet of seven ships, at last agreed to take him aboard. Standing on the beautiful Scandinavian shore, his smile was wide and he was certain no happier laddie ever was or ever would be again. He watched the other men wade into the crisp waters of the bay, toss their gear inside, turn around, lift themselves up until they could sit on the rim of the ship and then easily swing their legs over. It was something he had practiced several times and knew precisely how to do.

Why he failed he would never be quite certain, but he guessed it was because the boat he practiced on was smaller than his father's ship. He managed to toss his extra clothing, a heavy blanket, his warm cloak and even the shield his father had given him the night before into the ship. But when he tried to sit the rim, he was suddenly face down in the water. Just as abruptly, his father hauled him out – one hand grasping the back of his baggy brown long pants and the other taking hold of the back of his red tunic. Stefan was swiftly pulled aboard and abruptly dropped - leaving him wet, face down on the deck and completely humiliated amid roars of laughter and jeers from not only his father's men, but the crowd standing on the shore.

Humiliated indeed, but not enough to set aside his elation at being aboard, even when, none too gently, his father shoved him into a sitting position in the stern, warned him to stay there and took little notice of him for a long time after.

Stefan's father was named Donar after a Norse god of storms most no longer believed in. He had a square face with neatly trimmed facial hair and although his nose had obviously been broken more than once, it was straight and pointed, which all the woman agreed, made him exceedingly handsome. His long blond hair, sharp blue eyes, and height of nearly six and a half feet made him by far the strongest and the mightiest, which earned him the respect, if not the fear, of the other men.

As soon as his son was settled, Donar began barking orders. He needn't have bothered, for his men were well aware they were expected to be seated facing the stern on the narrow benches that lined both sides of the deck, holding their long oars straight up – which was exactly what they were doing.

It was a proud ship of oak wood carved upward at both the stern and the bow until it reached twice the height of the tallest man. The horn was carved into the fierce head of a dragon and faced outward to ward off sea monsters while the back represented the dragon's tail. Attached to each side of the ship's bow was the golden image of a fierce lion to ward off any animal dangers they might encounter on land.

The large ship could easily hold a hundred men, although Donar chose to take only sixty per ship. Fewer men meant more room for sleeping, supplies and any captives they happened to bring back. In preparation for each voyage there was much to consider and Donar ran a mental check list of supplies, which he always saw to the loading of himself. But when it came to enough food, he searched the face of the man seated to his right until Anundi understood his concern and nodded – they had ample food aboard and Donar's only son, his only living family, in fact, would not taste hunger on this voyage.

Satisfied his ship was ready, the commander took up a position near his son in the stern, took hold of the rudder post, raised his other hand high and looked across the water at the other ships in his fleet. Each man also held his oar straight up and was staring at his ship's stroke, who in turn impatiently watched Donar for the signal.

The race was about to begin.

It was the same each time they left shore and only once had another ship beaten Donar's crew out of the bay, through the narrow fjord and into the open waters of the North Sea. Some said he cheated, for his mooring was at least a hairs-breath closer to the fjord than the other ships. To prove them wrong, Donar had the *Sja Vinna* moved northward several feet and inwardly smiled.

Donar's men were not stronger or more skilled; it was his ship that gave him the advantage. All Viking ships had shallow hulls which enabled the men to beach the ship, strike and make good their escape with lightning speed. But the pride of the Viking fleet was fitted with a hull that was a good six inches shallower than the others, allowing just enough more speed and agility to win nearly every race.

Someday he would share that secret with his son. It was not cheating so much as it was a necessary challenge for the men, lest they grow lazy and incompetent. And it was good fun for all. Every man, woman and child came to watch and most hastened to place a wager or two, for or against the longship *Sja Vinna.*

Donar lowered his arm until it was straight out. In precise unison, all sixty men in each of ten ships set their oars in the water and got ready. Stefan's chest swelled with pride, for now he was not just another number in the crowd watching, but was himself aboard ship and about to taste the delights of the entire world. He had only a slight twinge of regret when he leaned out so he could see around the steep upward swing of the carved back and take one more look at the beloved aunt and uncle who raised him after his mother passed.

Then his father dropped his hand, gave a shout and the race began.

In every race it was at this very point that the winner and the losers were determined, for it was not enough to simply lower the oars in the water. They must be lowered at precisely the right angle so that when the shout was given, the men could immediately pull with enormous force at the same moment and the same angle, lift the oars, put them back in the water and pull again in perfect harmony. It was a skill they practiced often at sea.

Not at all his first time on the ocean, Stefan knew enough to hang on, but he did not expect the profound jerk sixty powerful men could create. He lost his grip and went tumbling forward. But then the oars were lifted, which stopped his momentum and he rolled back. It took him two more attempts to get himself upright long enough to grab hold of anything at all, which happened to be an ax handle with the blade driven hard into the deck.

He quickly looked up to see if his father had noticed his blunder, and was relieved when the commander seemed only to care about the competition. Nevertheless, Stefan could not have been more chagrined for they were fast approaching the fjord and he had nearly missed the whole race.

He leaned out again to look back at the figures of his aunt and uncle growing smaller on the shore of his Scandinavian homeland. Then he looked to see where all the other ships were. The *Sja Vinna* was ahead, but not by much. He held his breath. Surely his first race would not be a loss. If it were, it would be a terrible omen, so much so his father might take him back home for fear of what it could mean.

But then the *Sja Vinna* shot ahead and when Stefan looked, a group of men standing as close to the high walls of the fjord as the flat land would allow, judged the winner of the race and held up Donar's colors of blue and gold.

It was such a short race the men were hardly winded, or so they would have the laddie believe, even though their tunics were completely soaked through with sweat. Thrilled, Stefan joined his triumphant shout to theirs. The race, what he saw of it, exhilarated him and already he was looking forward to returning home so he could boast of having won his first race.

No sooner had the thought passed through his mind than he turned his attention back to the ship and marveled at the way it glided over the smooth blue water of the fjord. Seven of the ten ships dropped back, but he was expecting that. Donar wanted only two ships to accompany the *Sja Vinna* on this voyage. Even after they passed successfully between the two foliage covered high cliffs with cascading waterfalls, the men continued to row, although at a less urgent pace.

At last they entered the North Sea and conquered the first few waves before Donar shouted, "Stow yer oars and set yer shields lads!"

Their precision was remarkable as one by one each man lifted his oar, set it inside and then hung his colorful shield over the side facing out.

Stefan watched his father give charge of the rudder to Anundi, and then hang his son's shield next to his own on the port side. Then his father shouted the order Stefan most wanted to hear. "Set yer sail, lads.

It was a monstrous wooden mast made of the same sturdy oak as the ship and set just a bit off center, with a thin golden image of a bird at the top that moved according to the direction of the wind. The massive square sail was as tall as the ship was long and would be used as a tent when the rains came, as surely they would. Made of thickly woven, off-white hemp, the sail was unfurled, hoisted to the top of the mast by several stout men and with a loud pop, the wind snapped the sail taut. As quickly as they could, the men secured the rigging to the ship sides, the bow and the stern.

Stefan's uncle had taken him out to sea a time or two, but only on a small boat fit for fishing. Fascinated, Stefan studied every inch of the sail, and watched exactly how everything was done. It was only after the sail was set, that he realized his father had walked the length of the ship and was now in the bow. He could only see his legs under the billowed bottom of the sail, his father said to stay put and Stefan knew not to disobey. But he sorely objected to such a barrier now that he could at last spend more than a day or two with his father.

"'Tis safer here, laddie, till ye've the hang o' it." said Anundi. Like all the men, Anundi Spörr was dressed well. He wore leather shoes, long pants with attached socks that insured warm legs and feet, a tunic and a floppy long-sleeve under tunic made of linen. The undergarment hung several inches below his red woolen outer tunic and was belted with a leather belt and a bronze buckle. Being able to wear linen, and more of it than necessary, especially if it was brightly embroidered or decorated with colorful cloth braids, which his was, signified great wealth.

All the Vikings brought back plunder and their families prospered because of it, but everyone said his father and Anundi were the wealthiest of the lot. An abundance of weapons was also a sign of wealth and the Vikings in his father's command had them all. They each had a long handled axe, a three-pronged spear with iron tips for killing and for fishing, a helmet with a nose protector, a sword, and a dagger. Anundi's sword had a gold plated handle and a wide, flat blade.

Now that the hard work of rowing was ended and there was a nip in the sea air, Anundi handed the rudder off to yet another man so he could put on his long, sheepskin cloak. Once he had it around his shoulders, he held a round, gold brooch steady at the neck, pinned the two layers of material together and then moved the opening to one side, freeing his sword and the hand needed to wield it.

It was the first real notice Stefan had taken of his father's longtime friend and second in command. He nodded his understanding and waited for Anundi to sit down beside him before he asked. "To where do we sail?"

"Scotland, laddie, Scotland – the land o' delights." His smile made the boy smile too. "Laddie, do ye intend to die this day?"

Stefan was shocked by the question. "Nay."

"Then ye best get out o' those wet clothes afore ye freeze solid."

*

Donar stood squarely in front of the long, dragon-shaped neck of the bow with his legs apart for balance. He folded his arms and nodded his approval to his men. He was pleased with winning the race and the precision with which they carried out their tasks. It was a sign of great respect for a man who wanted to impress the son he hardly knew.

His son, however, was even more inexperienced than he suspected and with the sail between them, he at last allowed himself to laugh at Stefan's ungainliness. "The laddie be none too steady," he whispered to the men nearest him. Soon he was joined in laughter, leaving Stefan puzzled as to what the joke might be. But the eyes near him left no doubt – they were laughing at him. No sooner had he concerned himself with that, than he was diverted by a dolphin in the water on its back beside the ship, eyeing him as though it too was laughing.

Stefan rolled his eyes and defiantly folded his arms.

He did not know why, but the boy suddenly leaned out and looked back at the land he was leaving behind. For a moment he feared he would never see it again, but he shook off the foreboding and continued to marvel at the diminishing size of the place he knew to be a beautiful, vast land with pleasant meadows, fine fishing and snowcapped mountains. He watched it for as long as he dared, then turned back to face his father.

All the men seemed to have a particular chore save him and he hoped he would not remain idle for the entire voyage. "What am I to do?"

Minding the rudder again, Anundi smiled. "Yer father wants ye to watch, listen and learn. There'll be work aplenty afore long."

That too made Stefan happy. He wanted to be a part of them, not a guest aboard their magnificent ship. Yet the foreboding that he may never see home again returned twice more. He spoke not a word of it for fear the men would think him childish and weak. He simply could not risk their bad opinion of him, not now, not when he was so close to becoming what he dreamed of being – a Viking.

It was a decision he would regret the rest of his life.

CHAPTER II

It was Anundi who would do most of the teaching and the first lesson was to make it from one end of the ship to the other without stepping on anyone or falling overboard. He explained how to either slip under the sail or hold on to it and swing out to reach the other side. Stefan chose the latter. The first couple of times, he nearly fell overboard, but with a little more practice, he excelled and his father was pleased, not so much that he had mastered it but that he was willing to try.

For the remainder of the day, the boy watched the men adjust the sail according to the wind, watch for sea monsters or unfriendly ships, sharpen their swords and break out the food for their evening meal. Then as the sun began to set, they lowered the sail, stowed it, dropped anchor and began to settle in for the night.

It was not until after the rest of the men were settled that Donar motioned for his son to join him in the bow. Both wore their warm cloaks and as they sat down, Donar reached for his son's blanket and handed it to him. "I am pleased to have ye with me, Stefan. I have dreamed o' it often."

Stefan's jaw dropped, "Ye would have taken me to sea even without all me beg'n?"

"Aye, but I enjoyed yer beg'n. As soon as ye learned to speak ye began to demand it. When ye were five, ye threatened to kill me if I dinna take ye."

Stefan smiled. "I meant it too."

Donar scooted back until he could comfortably lean against the large cloth sacks stowed in the bow. "For these many years ye have had questions and I have had no time to answer them. Now there be the time…ask, my son."

Stefan had to think about it for a moment. There were thousands of questions, or at least seemed to be, but he could only think of one just now. "I want to know…"

"Go on, I will answer any question ye ask."

"Ye will think me still a wee laddie."

"If ye are, the fault be mine for not having helped ye become a lad."

Stefan quickly glanced at the exhausted men laying between the benches and taking up every inch of available space on the deck. Only four of them were still sitting upright with their eyes held out watching for other ships and the dreaded sea monsters.

"'Tis that my aunt will not speak o' her and I dinna even know my mother's name."

"Ah, well yer aunt loved her sister very much and 'tis painful to speak o' her. 'Twas painful for me too, but I dinna mean to neglect telling ye about yer mother. Her name was Sheena and she asked me to give ye this." He tossed one side of his cloak over his shoulder, found the thin strap around his neck and pulled a pouch out from inside his tunic. All the men wore small pouches to carry a scrap of clean cloth, coins, flint, tinder and a small piece of "c" shaped metal with which to strike the flint. But Donar's pouch was larger and from it, he withdrew a gold medallion.

Stefan's eyes grew wide. "Never have I seen such a treasure." He leaned forward so his father could slip the long leather string over his head and then lifted the medallion with his hand to study its beauty.

"Scotland has many great treasures. This was a gift to yer mother from her father." He watched the boy admire the medallion for a while longer and then decided he might as well tell him all of it. "Yer mother made me promise not to let ye go to sea."

Stefan was stunned, "Why?"

"Because she loved me."

"I dinna understand."

"Then I will explain it. She was the most beautiful lass I have ever seen. Ye have her eyes, I think, and her shade o' yellow hair. Sometimes, particularly when something dinna please ye, ye look exactly like I remember her when she was riled." Donar paused to take a breath. "I love her still and there be not a day goes by I dinna think o' her."

"Ye were not there when she died."

Donar winced at the pain his son's words brought. "I stayed away too long and yer mother was already in the ground by the time I came back, she and the bairn with her. 'Twas a daughter, or so the seer said. Yer aunt swore she would never forgive me for that as well as the other, but she did agree to keep ye until ye were grown. Ye were treated well?"

"Aye, very well. What other?"

Donar smiled at the memory, took a deep breath and slowly let it out. "It was a glorious battle, the best I have ever seen. The Scots put up a fierce fight and we might have lost had we not been better trained. Out o' the corner o' my eye, I saw a lass running from the village. I feared she would bring other forces against us, so I chased after her."

"Was it my mother?"

"It was."

"She was Scottish?"

"To the bone. Did yer aunt not teach ye Gaelic?"

"Aye," Stefan answered with a smile. "'Tis not so different from our language."

"I too had a Scottish mother and we will practice it now. The lads dinna speak it and this way we will have privacy." He pulled up his sleeve, showed a scar and then pulled his cloak back around him for warmth. "When I laid hand on Sheena, she bit my arm hard and drew blood. I let go and she nearly escaped, but I grabbed her again and pulled her to the ground. She thought I meant to force her."

"Did ye?"

Again Donar smiled. "My mother made me take a pledge not to and I have honored that pledge. Mother dinna say, but as I grew up not looking at all like the man I called father, I believe she was forced." He paused, giving his son a little time to absorb the revelation. "The lad I called father was unkind, so when I was o' age I killed him and took to the sea."

"Did yer mother scorn ye for killing him?"

Donar nodded. "At first, but when I brought back gold and silver from England, I was quickly forgiven and in the end, she confessed she was grateful I killed him."

"Then I am pleased too."

"Aye, he deserved to die for what he did to her."

"What did he do to her?"

"Whatever he wanted. A lass who be forced has few choices. She, and the child if one be conceived, will starve if she dinna marry the first lad who will have her, even if she knows him to be unkind. For a lad, pleasuring himself takes but a few minutes. For the lass he forces, the misery dinna end until the day she dies." Again he kept quiet for a time, hoping his son was old enough to grasp the true meaning. "Now I will have yer pledge never to force a lass. Do ye give it?"

He waited for Stefan's nod and then continued. "As to yer mother, I held her to the ground, made her promise not to hurt me again and let her up. It was then I saw how beautiful she was and I believe it was then she began to love me."

"Because ye did not force her?"

"Aye, she said as much later. There was little time, so I picked her up and carried her toward the ship. When she realized what I was doing, she folded her arms and glared at me. 'I'll not go without me sister,' she said. I only meant to take her away from the fighting and talk her into going with me. But she told me which was her sister and then hid behind the rocks until I returned."

At first Stefan was astonished, but then he began to smile. "Ye took them both and for this my aunt hates ye."

"She does indeed. Sheena said she was pledged to marry a deceitful lad and if I wanted her, I had to spare her sister a dreadful marriage."

"But my aunt dinna see that?"

"Nay, she believed she was in love. Even now that she loves her husband very well, she still thinks I robbed her o' the life she was to have. Her betrothed was a laird and she would have been his mistress."

"His miserable mistress."

"True. A lad must learn to know what be best for those he cares about. He must be stronger and wiser even when everyone else disagrees." Donar studied the worried look on his son's face for a moment, found a more comfortable sleeping position and closed his eye. "Fret not, I will teach ye."

*

Stefan did not keep count but believed crossing the sea took more than a month. His days were spent sailing, watching for sea monsters, learning to row in sync when the wind was slack, eating and sometimes slipping over the side to bathe in the ocean. He learned to read the stars and to discern the placement of the sun by watching the shadow cast beneath a round disk affixed to the top of an iron peg in the deck. His chores included taking a flask of water from man to man quenching their unrelenting thirst and seeing that not a drop was wasted. His was also to open the water barrels to catch the rain during storms.

In times of lull when the wind was lax and the men tired of rowing, they delighted in telling Stefan stories about the years of Viking conquests in places as far away as North Africa and the Middle East. They described fierce battles, the weapons used against them and how they managed to stay alive. Yet they all agreed the plight of the Vikings was becoming more dangerous and less rewarding, which was why they preferred destinations closer to home.

Invariably, the discussion turned to a debate between the men who preferred a plump lass to a thin one, and then to the abilities and attributes of all women, half of which Stefan was not at all certain he believed. Occasionally, he looked to his father to see the truth of it and welcomed his slight nod or the shake of his head.

After that, the men struck a more somber note as they remembered the fallen and told of carving their names in the Snoleved Stones back home so eternity would remember them.

It all sounded glorious and Stefan was mesmerized. But when he and his father spoke Gaelic, Donar was careful to tell his son the truth about war, death and dying in great detail so he would not find it quite so enchanting. "A lad must know what be worth dying for and what be not. Wealth be not."

Stefan wrinkled his brow, "But we are Vikings."

"We are lads afore we are Vikings. Only the protection of yer family be worth dying for. Everything else comes and goes like the tide. Today yer wealthy, tomorrow yer wife dies and ye have wasted yer life trying to bring her treasures – when all she wanted was more time with the lad she loved." He crossed himself in his wife's memory and then looked up at the brightest star. "Soon ye will see Scotland. Many a Viking lives in Scotland and so will we."

"What?" Stefan swallowed hard. "Why?"

"Because I promised yer mother. The only way to prevent ye from going to sea be to let the ships leave without us."

"But father…"

"Stefan, ye dinna have my rage and rage be what it takes for a Viking to stay alive. Ye are a gentle soul with yer mother's kindness. I would have ye live free o' war, loving a good lass and giving me lots o' grandsons. Do ye agree?"

Stefan did not agree. His mind was filled with the excitement of fierce battles, women and plunder. But he loved his father and so he reluctantly relented with the slightest of nods.

For three days, the men used the sail to shield themselves from driving rain while a massive storm tossed the ship around. If they were to be eaten by sea monsters, a storm was the most dangerous time and all the men worried – all but Stefan, who would have been delighted to see at least one.

On the fourth day, the heavy fog lifted, the sun broke through the clouds and Donar was relieved to see they had not lost a single ship. They were, however, off course. He studied the disk shadow on the deck, corrected their course and headed them once again toward Scotland.

When he could, Stefan stood in the stern hoping to be the first to sight land. Like most of the men, he wore a braid on each side of his face and then tied the two together in the back with twine to keep his long hair out of his eyes. He wore his dagger, sword and sheath proudly. His boots that laced up the sides were nearly too small, but it meant he was still growing and that was a good thing, especially for a Viking.

Being a Viking was a dream he had not yet given up. He fervently hoped his father would change his mind, perhaps when he saw how completely boring living on land day after day could be. He hardly paid attention when his father came to stand next to him, but when Donar pointed to a bird, Stefan took notice.

"The gulls tell us we are near land." Donar pulled another string from around his neck, put it over his son's head and dropped the heavy pouch inside his son's tunic. "They will expect me to have this instead o' ye. We will trick them." He winked and then folded his arms. "When the commander o' a ship dies, he be put out to sea and the ship set afire." He playfully nudged Stefan and leaned a little closer. "'Tis a waste o' a good ship."

Stefan smiled and went back to keeping a sharp eye out for land. The death of his commander was not something he wanted to contemplate now…or ever.

CHAPTER III

Kannak needed a husband.

She did not want one and was not at all convinced she would know what to do with one, but now that her father neglected to return, life promised to be extremely difficult for a mother and daughter trying to survive alone. Marriage was Kannak's idea and her mother flatly refused to consider it, but in the end Kannak could think of no other answer.

There were stipulations of course, for the two had talked of the man she would marry. "See that he has the strength of an ox, does not take to strong drink and has good teeth," her mother instructed. As she mounted her horse, Kannak wondered just how she could ask a man to show his teeth before she married him. But she decided she would puzzle that out later.

They were members of Clan Macoran and lived in a cottage on the north side of the river that separated clan Macoran from Clan Limond. Clan Macoran's land lay in a wide "*L*" shape at the foot of the gradual slope of a high hill. Small farms dotted the longer part of the bend that bordered the river while the other end stretched north along the eastern coast of Scotland. Clan Limond owned the flatter land to the south of the river.

For the most part, the two clans were peaceful, although there were disputes from time to time over livestock, fishing and women. Mostly they fought over the salmon in the river but sometimes over women, of which there never seemed to be enough. Women died in childbirth and men died in battle, but when there were as few wars as there had been lately, the men outlived two and sometimes three wives.

Kannak wore her long, auburn hair in a loose braid down the middle of her back and for this occasion, she looked as best she could in her woolen, ankle-length, unbelted frock. It was a pale gray with wide sleeves and since it was such a special occasion, she also wore a long under shirt of soft linen. The under garment was a gift from her uncle who lived in the far north. Her shoes were clean, her face scrubbed and she guessed that would have to be enough to attract a husband.

She considered herself to be exceptionally strong of heart and mind, but as she turned her horse and rode away, a sickness stirred in her stomach. She was, after all, but thirteen years of age and had not considered taking a husband so soon. Her mother's description of how children were conceived served to increase her anxiety and that too she wanted desperately to consider later.

But she simply could think of no other way. It was spring and their small plot of land needed more tending than two women could manage. Even if they could manage alone, they could not grow enough extra grain, barley or peas to trade for necessities such as salt, tools and weapons.

It was of weapons they were most concerned. Her father had taken them all when he left, except for a long bow neither of them was strong enough to draw. Her father normally bartered their cheese, milk and eggs for what they needed. But such small offerings were not enough to gain the gold and silver coins with which to pay the smithy for sound weapons. Therefore, Kannak needed a husband. Only a husband who brought his own weapons to the marriage could protect them.

Instead of following the path along the edge of the river that would take her around the wide bend to the village, Kannak decided to ride up the gradual slope through the trees to the top of the high land that overlooked both the home of her clan, the shore and the magnificent ocean beyond.

As always, when she reached the top, the sight of the endless water and the smell of the fresh sea air took her breath away. Looking at the ocean was the thing she loved most and she was tempted to just sit her horse and spend the rest of the day watching the waves crashing against the rocks. She was about to head down the other side of the hill to the village when she paused to reconsider. Surely there was another way.

There was one other option, but she dared not consider it – she could tell Laird Macoran of their troubles. Once it was clear her father was not coming back, she suggested they ask Laird Macoran for help. Her mother flatly refused and said it so sternly, Kannak did not argue. But just now she was tempted to risk her mother's ire. It was, after all, the duty of the laird to see that all the members of the clan were well taken care of. Besides, Jirvel was likely to be just as enraged when she returned with a husband.

Kannak sighed and watched a seagull glide out over the ocean. The air smelled fresh, a gentle breeze made the leaves in the trees rustle and it was such a pleasant day, she had to force herself to think clearly – take a husband or tell Laird Macoran? How was she ever to make the right decision?

*

It was midmorning when the Vikings spotted land. A small village was also coming into view which meant they would not have to sail north or south to find one. It would also be an easy mark for only three Viking ships. If the wind continued to blow steady as it was now, they could strike and be on their way back before dark. The men quickly gathered their weapons, put off their cloaks, donned their head gear and made ready to row. The mood aboard ship was a mixture of excitement and contemplation during which Stefan gained the advice of nearly every man. "Yer land legs'll deceive ye, laddie…find a plump lass…dare not turn yer back on a Scot…"

But then the men began to row to the mark of the stroke and the closer they got to land, the stronger Stefan's foreboding became. The village was set well back, which meant the Vikings had to run up the beach, climb several rocks and cover more open ground to reach the village. Surely the Scots would try to strike them down before they got over the rocks.

The mark of the stroke kept a steady beat, but Stefan's heart was pounding three times faster. There were no Scots coming to fight them on the shore and he saw only two women running from the village in an effort to hide themselves and their children. This was nothing at all like the glorious tales told nightly of the Viking men fighting and dying at the water's edge.

Standing in the stern of the ship, Stefan studied his father's face, but Donar was calm and had an air of confidence about him as though he was certain the Vikings could survive anything the Scots could throw at them. He had not even put on his helmet with the nose protector, therefore Stefan did not put his on either. If his father believed it, then Stefan was willing to believe it as well. Stefan did, however, check the position of the sword and dagger tied around his waist repeatedly.

What the Vikings preferred was hand to hand combat, mainly the use of their long handled axes, but on the shore of Scotland, clan Macoran preferred something a little less one-on-one. Hidden in every place it was possible for a man to hide, they waited until the boats docked and the invaders began to jump from the ships before they loaded their arrows and drew their bow strings back.

Stefan was certain the greatest longships carrying the greatest commander and the best trained Viking warriors in the world were that day heading into a trap. But if Donar suspected the same, he did not let on, turn his ships back, or even slow their pace.

The Vikings beached the longships in the sand with a forceful thud that surprised Stefan and he almost lost his balance. The men in the bow of the ship jumped to the ground first and Stefan was right in line behind them. As soon as the man in front of him jumped, so did Stefan. But after weeks at sea, his knees buckled when he hit the hard sand and he feared he'd broken both his legs.

In his excitement, he forgot to get his shield and Stefan was about to draw his sword when his father grabbed hold of his arm and began to pull him down the shore away from the river, away from the village and away from the battle. "Run!" he heard Donar shout.

*

It was not really Kannak's horse. In fact, she had no idea where the horse came from. The day before, it just showed up. It had a shiny coat as black as night, a black mane and tail and there was not a mark of any other color anywhere, not even a touch of white on his nose. It held its head high and beyond a doubt it was the most beautiful stallion she had ever seen. Kannak was certain it belonged to a wealthy laird or perhaps the King of Scotland who would come looking for it. But no one had come as yet, therefore the horse was hers as much as it was anyone's.

Their old horse was yet another thing her father took with him, together with their only saddle and bridle. When the stallion walked down the path to their cottage, Kannak had no way to capture it without a bridle. But to her amazement, the horse stood still, let her get a running start, grab a handful of mane and swing up. She ignored her mother's worry, rode him all around the property and discovered if she patted the side of his neck twice, the horse would stop. When night came she feared the stallion would be gone by morning, but he was not and she was delighted.

It was then, seated on the stallion on the crest of the hill, that she realized there must be some sort of fight in the village below. The village did not appear to be on fire, for there was no more smoke than the normal outside fires produced, but she thought she could…no she absolutely could hear the clash of swords and the shouts of men. She moved the horse to another vantage point and one look at the shore told her everything she needed to know.

"The Viking dogs are back," she breathed. Three deserted Viking ships were run aground on the shore. "Now what do I do?" She raised her eyes to the peaceful blue sky and said a silent prayer. The answer to her prayer, she was to discover, would soon be running up the hill toward her.

*

"Run," his father shouted again. Stefan was so terrified of being shot in the back, he need not be told to run. It was a terror that would not leave him all the days of his life. Moments before, as they ran down the sandy beach from the ship, a barrage of arrows began whizzing past them from behind. He felt Donar grab his arm a second time, pull him over the rocks toward the trees at the bottom of a hill and then shove him ahead. Running as fast as he could, he darted through the trees, found a path and kept running uphill until he realized he could no longer hear his father behind him. He quickly glanced back, spotted Donar on the ground and stopped.

He could hear the Scots shouting and growing closer, but he ignored them. His father lay on his side with one arm outstretched as if reaching for his son and Donar wasn't moving. Stefan hurried back, knelt down, put his hand on his father's shoulder and then noticed the arrow sticking out of the middle of his father's back. Blood covered most of Donar's backside and was still trickling out of the jagged wound. "Nay, father," he whispered, but when he looked, the life was already gone from Donar's eyes.

He looked for his father's red and gold shield, but it was nowhere in sight. Then he thought to remove his father's sword and sheath, but he could hear the men's shouts getting louder, knew they were coming his way and his fear won out. Quickly, he lovingly touched his father's head, grabbed Donar's long handled, three-pronged spear, got up and ran back up the hill.

The Scots were getting closer but his long legs and youth gave him a slight advantage. In the small clearing at the top, he spotted a girl on a horse, put a finger to his lips, prayed she would not tell on him, and looked for a place to hide. The trees were too narrow and too far apart to conceal him and the only place he could find was a rock not quite large enough. He ran to it, crouched down and tried to slow his breathing. Soon he realized there was no place to hide the spear, so he tossed it away. Then, to his amazement, the girl positioned her horse between him and the Scots.

Two men with red hair and drawn swords burst through the trees and were surprised to see Kannak. They stopped to catch their breath for a moment and then looked around. "Did a Viking come this way, lassie?"

Kannak widened her eyes. "A Viking!" She quickly crossed herself. "May God protect us."

It was enough of an answer. One of the men muttered as he led the other one away, "I could have sworn I saw two."

She waited until she could no longer see or hear the Scots and motioned for the boy to come to her. She watched him recover his spear, climb up on the rock and then felt him mount behind her. A second later she urged the horse forward.

But they had only made it to another small clearing when Stefan slipped his legs under hers so she could not kick the side of the horse, pinned her arms with his free arm and said, "Stad."

The horse halted at the stranger's command and at first Kannak was only taken aback, but then she became frightened. The Viking was surprisingly strong and in her haste to solve her problem, she had not considered having to fight him.

Stefan felt her tremble, put his mouth close to her ear and

whispered, "I will not harm ye."

He spoke her language and it comforted her enough to let her relax against him. Just as Stefan did, Kannak turned to look through the trees at what was happening on the shore below.

His father's ship was still beached in the sand, but in the other two ships the Vikings had their oars in the water and were swiftly rowing away. His father's men, his cherished Vikings, the men he called friends, were leaving his father's body and their commander's son behind. It was a sight he could never have imagined seeing and it took a while to accept the truth of it. Slowly, he moved his legs back and released his grip on the girl's arms.

Just as slowly, Kannak nudged the horse's flanks and turned them toward home. She was relieved. He promised not to harm her and so far, his word was good. Perhaps not all Vikings were vicious, murdering dogs after all. All she had to do now was convince her mother of that. She waited until they were well away before she spoke. "What be yer name?"

The hurt in Stefan's heart was so overwhelming all he wanted to do was bellow his rage and keep bellowing until his sorrow subsided. But he did not. He kept quiet, not trusting himself to speak for fear he would cry out – or worse, weep like a child.

"Never mind yer name, then. How good are ye at lying?" Kannak covered her mouth to stifle a giggle. "What am I saying? Everyone knows a word from the mouth o' a Viking be bound to be a lie." Then she got somber again. "Taking ye home will not be easy, not without a lie, that is. Let me think. We will say ye have come from my uncle in the north to help us work the land. Aye, I think she will believe it; we truly do have family in the north. We can offer ye a warm bed and whatever food we manage to have, which be very little at the moment."

She paused just to see if he cared to contribute to the conversation, but he did not. "There be the tithe, ye see. The priest has promised eternal damnation o' our very souls if we dinna pay. Never have I heard o' anyone refusing, although sorely I am tempted to be the first. On the other hand, if we dinna have food soon, it will be we who must go to the priests and beg for a meal or two. The priests will not deny us, not if they deem us truly hungry."

Again she waited. Again he said nothing. At last they reached the bottom of the hill and turned down the path that led away from the village. "The muddle o' it be, we have no weapons to hunt with. It be spring, we have eaten our winter store and we need a man to help us. First, we must do something about yer hair."

"What be wrong with my hair?"

Kannak smiled. "Ye look like a Viking. Scotsmen dinna wear their hair that long." She patted the side of the horse's neck to halt him and swung her leg over so she could sit sideways. Kannak folded her hands in her lap and took a long look at Stefan's face. "Ye are but a laddie. Oh well, ye will have to do. I say we make our bargain now. I have saved yer life. In return, ye will save ours."

It was not an unreasonable request, he thought. What she said was true, she did save his life and where else could he go? But he could not believe the Vikings would not come back for him. He imagined them sailing only to the horizon and then coming back...perhaps tomorrow. "I will think on it."

"And that be the best I can hope for...ye will think on it?"

"Aye."

"I see." Kannak glared at him. "At least I will not have to marry ye."

"I dinna want a wife."

"Well bletherskite, I dinna want a husband either." She tilted her head and suspiciously eyed him. "How be it ye speak my language?"

"My mother was a Scot."

"Fancy that, bletherskite, so be my mother."

The last thing in the world he felt like doing was smiling, but this little slip of a girl with a face overrun by freckles and dimples calling *him* a silly talker, was making him do just that. "I am Stefan."

"Stefan…it be a Viking name, but I have heard it afore. My father named me Kannak."

"A Viking name?"

Both her eyebrows shot up, "Ye know this name? Be it truly a Viking name?" She watched his eyes and nearly forgot to draw breath until his mouth began to curve into a smile. "Ye are lying."

"All Vikings lie, ye said so yerself."

"That I did." She grabbed hold of his arm and slid down off the horse. "Come with me to the river and I will cut yer hair. Ye have a blade, do ye not?"

CHAPTER IV

When they arrived at the small plot of land with one cow, two chickens and a garden that needed tending, Stefan had shoulder length hair, no braids and no belt around the outside of his tunic. Scots, particularly Scots who worked the land, could not afford leather belts and Kannak's mother was sure to be suspicious. He helped her down, dismounted and then watched her go into the small cottage and close the door.

Finally, Stefan had a moment to himself and he stroked the side of the horse's neck as if to draw comfort from the animal. His mind was spinning and when he leaned his forehead against the horse and closed his eyes, he could still see the image of his father's lifeless face. It was all he could do to keep from crying, but he held back his tears just as he knew his father would expect him to.

He should go back, he thought, for who was there to bury the Viking commander? Would the Scots give him a Christian burial; would they defile him somehow in their rage or would they leave his body to rot where it lay? Not knowing was more than he could abide and he had to go back. With one swift movement, Stefan swung back up on the horse and rode away. He only slightly heard Kannak screaming his name behind him.

*

It was almost dark when he slid down off the horse, crept back down the hill toward the village and looked for his father's body. Blood yet stained the ground, but his body was gone. There were marks in the dirt, a sure sign that the body had been dragged and cautiously Stefan followed the marks, mindful to stay out of sight of the village.

But then he felt a foreboding and went back. He didn't expect it, but the horse was right where he left him and when he mounted not knowing where to go, he let the stallion take him back to the same spot where he watched his Vikings row away. On the shore were men holding torches and the bodies of several Vikings lay side by side in his father's abandoned ship. The remains had been carefully laid out on the deck, each surrounded by dry straw. Their arms were crossed over their chests, and a measure of cloth lay over their faces just as their own families would have done.

A priest appeared to be giving last rites as the Scots shoved the ship away from the shore. Then three Scotsmen tossed in their torches and set it on fire.

It was a fitting burial for his father and because of it, the anger he felt for the Scots who had taken his father's life began to subside. He wondered, if only for a moment, if the Norsemen would have been so considerate of men who came to murder and plunder in their land. He wondered too if the Vikings would carve a stone in his father's memory when they got home. Surely they would and someday he hoped to see it.

He raised his gaze to the horizon and tried to see if the ships were still there, waiting until after dark to land and look for him. But they were gone and then he remembered his father's words: "Yer mother made me promise not to let ye go to sea."

Still he stayed, seated on the magnificent black horse on the crest of the hill until the last lick of flame was quenched and the ship sunk. He wanted to and thought he should cry, but now the tears would not come. Perhaps in the few short days he had with his father, he had become a man after all.

*

"Ye brought us a Viking, Kannak, and now the horse be gone." In the darkness of the cottage, Jirvel stood in the doorway to her bedchamber, took a deep breath and tried to hold back her ire.

"He agreed to help us."

"And ye believed him? He be a Viking, Kannak."

She hung her head. "I am sorry, mother. I will walk to the village for what we need tomorrow." Kannak could not stand to hear the hurt in her mother's voice, sat down on her bed and took off her shoes. "I am too hungry to think. Is there nothing to eat?"

"Milk."

"I am sick o' milk and cheese. Be there nothing more?"

"Not unless we kill a chicken."

It was useless. The chickens only laid one egg a day as it was; killing one meant fewer eggs to eat by half and that would only make things worse. She stretched out on the bed, pulled her cover up and closed her eyes. "I will think o' a way out o' our troubles tomorrow."

*

By the time the horse took Stefan back to the cottage, the candle light had been extinguished and it was dark inside. He quietly dismounted and watched the horse wander off, then tried to find a place to sleep for the night. In the dim moonlight, he spotted a structure that was little more than a roof, a back wall and two posts holding up the front of the roof. He moved some baskets out of the way and sat down.

Yet with no cover to keep him warm and a thousand thoughts running through his mind, sleep avoided him. He remembered the pouch filled with coins, pulled it out from under his tunic and examined the contents. He removed two coins, dug a hole near one of the front posts and buried the pouch. Then there was nothing to do but wait for dawn, which would come early this far north, just as it did in Norway. Soon he would find it difficult to go to sleep in the daylight, but for now a short night would be a blessing. And while he waited for dawn, he realized that somewhere in the middle of the ocean, he turned fifteen.

*

She was dreaming; she had to be. The glorious smell coming from the pot placed directly in the embers of the fire in the hearth was so magnificent, she dared not open her eyes for fear it would dissipate into a mist so light a breeze could carry it away.

"Kannak, wake up. He be back and we have food."

She dared to open one eye and then slowly opened the other. The magnificent smell was not a dream and she could not help licking her lips in anticipation. Then she spotted Stefan sitting at the table watching her with a grin on his face.

"Wake up, wee bairn," he said.

Annoyed at being called a baby, she abruptly sat up and glared. "From which o' our neighbors did ye steal this food?"

Stefan's grin turned to a scowl of his own. "I neglected to ask his name."

"Ye have brought a curse down upon us. There be a penalty in our clan for stealing and we will all be dead afore the noon meal."

"If that be the case, I suggest we eat all the evidence."

Jirvel was a striking woman at twenty-nine with her daughter's same color of hair, although her eyes were blue and the years of hard work had robbed her of her youth. As her daughter did, she wore a long, gray striped unbelted frock made of wool.

It was Jirvel's custom to watch and listen to people before she made up her mind to like them and so far, she believed she was going to like Stefan very much. He had, after all, come back, he looked to be a strong boy and he had weapons. Already she felt safer.

She turned the hot bread over once more in the pot, poked a hole in it to make sure it was done and reached for a bowl. The boy had a way about him that was pleasant and she was enjoying their banter. Stefan was exactly what her daughter needed. With no siblings, the girl had gotten away with far too much for far too long.

"Ye admit ye stole it then?" Kannak asked, putting on one shoe and then the other.

Stefan rolled his eyes. He picked the two gold coins up off the table and showed them to her. The wheat for the bread be yer store for the planting and with this ye can barter for better seed and enough to feed us until the harvest."

"Where did ye get those?"

"If ye must know, wee bairn, I found them."

"Bletherskite." She did not believe a word of it. "They are English coins. Next ye will say ye favor the English. We dinna prefer them."

"Nor do we?"

Kannak lightly bit her bottom lip and thought for a moment. "If we both hate the English, perhaps…"

Jirvel knew her daughter well enough to know Kannak would soon be challenging the boy, for what the girl loved most was competition and a good wager. "I suggest we eat and then see to the chores. There will be time for talking later."

The cottage was a pleasant place, not so different from the home he grew up in, except it was much smaller and square instead of oval shaped. It had the pleasant smell of lavender and spices. A small table and three chairs were on one side of the room and Kannak's bed was on the other. Several pots made of metal and baskets of different shapes and sizes were lined up near the walls, some obviously still in the process of being crafted. A small pile of heather sticks lay next to the hearth to use for fire wood and a doorway led to a second small room where he guessed Jirvel slept.

There were places on the wall to hang weapons, but the places were empty save for a long bow. Soon the bread got his attention and the smell of it made him want to lick his lips too. After the tasteless meals at sea, he was ready to devour all she could make. "Where be yer father?"

He directed his question to Kannak, but it was Jirvel who answered. "Eogan has gone off to war these three weeks and we have had no word of him." She put the bread in a bowl and set it on the table. "Kannak says ye agreed to stay and help us. Is it true?"

Stefan nodded, tore off a small piece of the hot bread, blew on it and quickly devoured it. Then he turned his attention back to the longbow. "In my…at home I tended my aunt and uncle's land. I am accustomed to it."

Kannak rolled her eyes. "She knows yer a Viking; she dinna believe the lie."

He stood up and took the longbow off the hook on the wall. Effortlessly, he pulled the string back to test it. "Then she has far more wits about her than her daughter."

Thoroughly insulted, Kannak stood up, straightened her frock and then put her hands on her hips. "Ye might as well put that back. Everyone knows Vikings go to sea and none are skilled enough to hunt on land. I wager yer the same."

Stefan didn't even bother to look at her. "What will ye wager?"

"Well…if ye win, I will haul all the water for two days."

"And if ye win?"

"Ye will milk the cow, morning and night, for two days."

"Lads dinna milk cows."

"Then I am fortunate yer not yet a lad." Kannak tore off two pieces of bread and walked out the door.

Jirvel watched him test the bow again and smiled. "God has surly sent ye to us, Stefan. Will my daughter lose her wager?"

"Aye."

"Good. She needs to be set down occasionally. Spend the day hunting while we see to the marketing. The land can wait another day or two and we must keep ye strong."

*

In the light of morning, Stefan got his first good look at the land. The cottage was far enough from the tree lined river to avoid the spring floods, yet close enough for fishing and hauling water. He followed the path to the river, knelt down, cupped his hands and splashed water on his face. But when he looked at the reflection, all he saw was his father's lifeless face. He closed his eyes tight, searched his mind for a pleasing image to remember and settled on the mighty commander standing in the stern of the ship with his legs apart and his arms folded. Finally daring to open his eyes and look again, the reflection he saw was his own. He looked as tired as he felt.

Stefan ran his fingers through his short hair and got up. Then he looked in all directions, decided he was alone, stripped down and took a quick bath in the cold water. It helped refresh him.

When he went back up the path, he paused a moment to admire the beautiful oak tree next to the cottage, with its sturdy branches and leaves enough to provide ample shade on hot days. Other oak trees and bushes lined all four sides of the property except where animals had trampled paths to the river over the years. In the middle was the farm land and it was obvious most had not been worked in years. He walked to the small garden, picked up a handful of dirt and let it run through his fingers. The soil was not so different from his home, nor was the climate, which so far, was just as warm if not warmer than home.

Once she was done with the milking, he let Kannak show him where everything was, helped both women mount the horse and then handed them the empty baskets and two flasks filled with fresh milk. After they were gone, he looked over the garden again and took stock of the tools in the shed. There weren't many and the wooden shovel was warped, but with good care, and if the weather was not too harsh, he thought he could manage to grow enough to feed them with perhaps a little extra.

At least the heather was a good source of food for the livestock, what little livestock there was. Heather had a thousand other uses, most of which the Scots took advantage of, he noticed. From it they made baskets with straps to hang over the back of a horse, baskets for carrying sheared wool, for harvesting vegetables and even small baskets lined with cloth and hung by the fire in the cottage to keep their salt and spices dry. They also made brooms, brushes, floor mats and even woven paths across unstable soil.

Yet when the plants began to overgrow the land allowing wolves and red foxes to get close to the livestock, the only answer was a Muirburn. That took a good bit of watching, for fear the fire got out of control, and Stefan doubted the three of them could manage it without help.

It was not hard to figure out which basket was used for fishing, although it was clear to see the women owned no useable lines of twine or hooks. No wonder they were hungry. He vowed to show them how to hold a torch near the river's edge at night, draw the fish to it and spear them with a sword or spear. Then he realized they had neither and found Kannak's father despicable for leaving them so completely without.

It was a far cry from the life he imagined as a Viking, but he tried not to think about that. He would need shoes soon and all he owned, including his warm cloak, went down with the ship. There was much to do and keeping busy would at least take his mind off his sorrow. Stefan abruptly went back inside the cottage, got the long bow and found two arrows.

CHAPTER V

It was not unlike many of the villages in Scotland, with a two-story keep made of stone where their laird and his family lived. In front of the keep was a large courtyard with a short wall around most of it. The stables were just beyond the wall at one end, and the clan used the other end of the courtyard as a market place. Surrounding the keep and courtyard were cottages of various sizes, some new and some seemingly very old, but in good repair. With the hill behind the village, trees everywhere, the ocean in the front and the mouth of the river emptying into the sea to the south, Clan Macoran was a desirable place to live indeed.

For most of the farmers on the plots of land granted them by their laird, the harvest had been plentiful. Selling their food at this time of year, when most had eaten there winter stores, was the most profitable. After all, not all were farmers. There were candle makers, weavers, cobblers, tanners, the laird and his family, builders, warriors and the priests, all of whom came to the market to barter for food on a regular basis.

Jirvel kept one back and used the other coin to afford vegetables, fruit, wheat and precious life giving seeds of various kinds they would need for the planting. The fresh salmon was tempting, but she reminded herself they now had a boy who could fish for them.

The market was alive with buyers and sellers all touting their remarkable victory over the Vikings the day before. Only three dead Scots and twenty-six Vikings killed. "They won't be coming back here again anytime soon," they all agreed.

Kannak and Jirvel listened to all the gossip and nodded when appropriate. Then their laird arrived and Kannak held her breath. Everything that happened in the clan was Laird Macoran's business, whether her mother liked it or not. They had to tell him about Stefan and her mother was not an accomplished liar. Even so, Kannak knew enough to remain silent and let her mother do the talking.

"Good day to ye, Jirvel," Laird Macoran said. He waited for them to curtsy and then smiled his approval. He was a tall man with a dimple in his chin normally covered by his beard. His thick hair was a dark shade of red, as was his facial hair, and his eyes were green. He was a fair minded man who smiled often and nearly everyone loved him. Macoran was dressed in a skirt made of a dark green and light brown tapered pants with shoes that laced up his legs to just below his knees. It was a new form of dress which seemed to be sweeping across all of Scotland, or so the gossip reported. Nevertheless, some of the men found the new dress unfamiliar and still wore their baggy long pants.

Jirvel did not return Macoran's smile. "Have ye any word o' my husband?"

Laird Macoran wrinkled his brow. Jirvel's question meant there were now three men who had taken their leave without his knowledge and he was not pleased. "Nay, I have heard nothing. The two o' ye are alone then?"

"Quite, but ye needn't worry, we can manage."

"How?"

"Just now ye care about us?"

He looked disturbed by Jirvel's outburst, started to touch her arm and then drew his hand back. "I will send a lad…"

She suddenly realized others were listening and bowed her head. "Ye need not bother, my brother sent a laddie to work the land."

"Yer brother knows ye are alone?"

"Nay, he does not know. The laddie be unexpected and I am grateful to have the help."

"Then I am grateful too."

Laird Macoran and Jirvel held their eyes on each other longer than was normal. No one in the clan was as bold as her mother when it came to standing up to Laird Macoran, and never had Kannak seen Jirvel this forthcoming, at least not in public. Her mother had just told a lie, did it very well and Macoran seemed to believe her. Kannak was relieved. Yet there was something more…something unsaid between them and this was not the first time Kannak noticed.

Macoran also realized others were listening, glanced at the girl and thought to change the subject. "Kannak will soon be old enough to marry."

At this Jirvel's anger grew and she narrowed her eyes, "She be but twelve and an only child. She be not yet ready to marry."

"She was twelve last year." He studied the rage rising up in Jirvel's eyes and decided not to push his luck. "Perhaps not yet then. I will see this laddie o' yer'n when I ride the land next." He nodded and walked away.

Kannak said nothing as she helped her mother mount the horse and handed her a full basket. Then she got on behind her and accepted a basket one of the men handed her. He was an older man who held his eyes to hers so long it made her uncomfortable enough to turn her head away. She remembered to thank him, but was greatly relieved when her mother nudged the side of the horse.

They were half way home before Jirvel spoke. "Ye must not come to the village so often as afore. Soon the men will be asking for ye and I will not have ye married to a nothing o' a lad like yer father."

"Ye have never called him that afore."

"I have never been this angry afore. He left us, Kannak. and there was no need."

"All lads go off to war."

"What war? We heard nothing o' a war save the one with the Vikings yesterday and Macoran had no idea he was gone. Yer father has abandoned us and he will not be back."

It was not as though Kannak did not have these same thoughts, but it was surprising her mother would say it out loud. Of all the things Jirvel taught her, respect for her father no matter how drunk he got, was at the top of the list.

"Would Macoran kill him for leaving us?"

Jirvel closed her eyes for a moment. "I'd not like seeing that, but he did not have Macoran's leave to go. A laird must have complete control over his clan or there will be madness."

"Then father dare not come back, not now that Macoran knows."

"Aye, Eogan may not be helpful, but neither be he dim-witted."

Kannak lovingly put her head against her mother's back. "I do like seeing what others have crafted at the market."

"I know ye do. Perhaps Stefan can go with ye and keep the lads away, but ye must not come alone. I will not have ye married until ye are a fully grown lass."

*

By the time they got back, Stefan had a grouse and a rabbit cooking on an outside spit. Jirvel was thrilled, Kannak was not, but that didn't stop her from eating. The meat and an apple each filled their stomachs and all of them were tired enough to go to bed early.

Grinning, Stefan got up from the table and picked up a bucket made of oak staves, "We are in need o' more water."

Kannak slumped. Then she stood, twirled her hand in the air, mockingly curtsied to him, yanked the handle out of his hand and marched out the door. "Bletherskite."

Both Jirvel and Stefan laughed. After she was gone, Stefan sat back down at the table. "Will she be safe going to the river alone?"

"She has done it all her life save these past weeks. Once Eogan was gone, we did everything together."

"Is this clan at war?"

"Nay," Jirvel answered.

"Then whom do ye fear?"

"Any lad who might take advantage o' two lasses alone. Word will spread that yer here to protect us and we will again be safe."

He nodded his understanding and accepted the goblet of mead she handed him. It was a sweet drink, but he did not care for it that much, took only a sip and set it aside.

Jirvel smiled. The laddie was not going to take to strong drink and that was refreshing. She decided it was a good time to caution her new charge. "Stefan, when ye go to the river ye may well see Limonds on the other side. They will not attack ye, but we are not so very friendly with that clan."

"Why not?"

"'Tis a long dispute over the salmon. Limond accuses us of taking our catch from his side of the river." She saw the perplexed look on his face and could guess what he was thinking. "Laird Limond be an old lad with no family and there be no accounting for his suspicions. His men watch us, but they mean no harm normally. Nevertheless, we take only the fish we need."

"I see. I brought a spear."

"A Viking spear with three prongs?"

"Aye."

"Good, we will use it but ye must hide it. In the village they know one o' the Vikings got away."

"Where best can I hide it?"

"Bring it inside and lay it along the wall behind the baskets. No one will see it there." She studied his face for a moment and decided she should tell him about the battle. "As I said, we are not fond o' the Limond, nor they o' us…except when the Vikings come. For that, we fight together. We lost only three, the Vikings lost twenty-six."

He could not help but close his eyes and bow his head. It was a hard thing to hear, but he would rather hear it from her where he did not have to hide his sorrow. At length, he gathered his wits. "How did the Limond get across the river so quickly?"

"'Tis right dead brilliant how they do it. When ye go to the village ye will see a large raft on each side o' the river. The men board the raft, tie the ropes to arrows and shoot them across so the men on the other side can pull the raft over."

"'Tis brilliant."

"Aye, but it takes time and for this battle, they were slow in pulling them across. A few minutes more and the battle might have been lost."

Stefan nodded. It explained why there were no men to fight them on the shore and he made a mental note to search out these rafts and have a look. For now, however, he did not want to think about it anymore so he smiled to relieve her worry. "'Tis the past and best left behind."

*

Jirvel insisted Kannak sleep with her and gave him the bed in the other room near the door. It was perhaps not proper to let a boy not related stay inside, but she decided she would feel safer with him and his weapons inside where he could protect them…safer than she felt in weeks.

As soon as Kannak came back with the water, she sent her off to bed and handed Stefan an extra blanket. She went to the doorway that separated the two rooms and untied the cord that held up the curtain. "Good night."

He nodded, watched her lower the curtain and took off his shoes. He again considered the need for a new pair. He could afford the cobbler and was tempted, but with a Viking missing, letting the Scots know of his wealth would not be such a good idea. Shoes would have to wait. With no sleep the night before and with the pain of losing his father draining him of all emotion, he quickly fell into a deep sleep.

*

It was Friday week before Laird Macoran arrived with his guard to see the laddie Jirvel's brother sent from the north. Each of the clansmen had red, shoulder length hair, trimmed beards and wore dark green tunics tucked inside belted long pants. For a long moment, Macoran stared at Stefan., who stood just behind Kannak and her mother. "My lads swear one got away and *he* looks like a Viking."

"So do half the lads in the north," Jirvel reminded him. "He is a good laddie and a gift from God in our time of need." The reminder that he had not realized they were alone, and had not seen to her care as a good laird should, seemed to do the trick and Macoran took his eyes off the tall boy. Then he looked over the land.

Already they were starting to clear a sizeable plot beside the cottage and getting it ready for planting. The skins of two red deer were stretched tight on wooden frames and they had reinforced the shed with more poles along the sides so the roof would not collapse. Even the small courtyard in front of the cottage looked different, although he could not quite discern why. Then he realized Jirvel had started planting flowers next to the cottage.

Though he did not let on, Stefan was revolted. The guards kept looking at Kannak, which obviously agitated Jirvel, and Laird Macoran was wearing Anundi's sword with the gold plated handle. It meant Anundi was dead too, and Stefan looked away pretending to check on the cow. It galled him to see another man wearing it, even if he was a laird, and Stefan silently vowed to have that sword for himself someday.

"Eogan has not come back, I see. Perhaps 'tis time for a new husband," Laird Macoran said.

Jirvel's mouth dropped and it took a moment for her to gather her senses. “And commit bigamy? Would ye have the church excommunicate me?”

“I could have the priest set aside yer marriage.”

She eyed him suspiciously for a moment. “Say the truth o’ it.”

He should have known he could not pull the wool over her eyes. “Ye have me, I see. Two lads have asked for ye since ye last came to the village. As their laird, I am forced to consider it.”

She glanced at the other men and tried to remember her manners. “I am complimented they find me pleasing, but I will wait for my husband’s return.”

“He is not coming back and we both know it.” Macoran expected an argument, but Jirvel hung her head as though his words hurt. He watched her for a moment before he said, “I will mention it again when next I see ye. Perhaps by then a new husband will be more to yer liking.” He looked once more at Kannak and nodded. “The spring festival be set for Monday week.” He hoped the news would please Kannak and he was not disappointed. He returned the girl’s smile and then the laird of Clan Macoran turned his horse and led his guard away.

Jirvel waited until Stefan walked off and then leaned closer to her daughter. “For this festival, we will bind yer bosom and add more freckles to yer face.”

Kannak watched her mother go back inside the cottage and then hurried to catch up with Stefan. She had to run. He was already past the garden and headed down the path toward the river. “Did ye see it?”

“See what?”

“The way Laird Macoran looked at my mother. It be the same every time he comes, which be not so often, I admit. He be happy to see her and she be annoyed that he came. Once when my father was not at home, he came back without his guard, took her inside where I could not hear and they quarreled."

"Quarreled? About what?"

"I dinna know, but she was forlorn for days after." Kannak had to half run to stay up with Stefan's long strides. "Where are ye going?"

"To the river."

"What for?"

"To get away from ye."

CHAPTER VI

He found a place near the water amid the bushes where he was certain Kannak could not find him and sat down on the ground. He should have known Anundi was dead for he surely would have made the Vikings come back for Donar and his only son. Stefan was annoyed with himself for not having guessed he was dead or taken even a moment to mourn the loss of the other men. Who else was laid out on the deck of the *Sja Vinna* before it was burned and sent to a watery grave? He doubted he would ever know.

Though the image of his father's death did not plague him as much as it had the first few days, the ache was still there and being alone served only to increase it. She had the potential of becoming a real pest, but being around Kannak was better than facing his sorrow head on.

He was about to get up and go back, but in the distance, he heard voices and changed his mind. It was Jirvel's voice he heard first and there was a man with her. As the voices grew closer, he parted the bushes just enough to see that the man was Laird Macoran. He had come back just as Kannak said he did once before. Stefan should have made his presence known, but he did not do it in time and then it seemed too late.

"We had naught to eat," Jirvel said.

"Ye know very well I care about ye. Countless times I have ridden my horse up the path or sat upon the hill just to get a glimpse o' ye."

"And still ye did not see we were alone?"

"Eogan be rarely where I can see him. He hides so I will not see him drunk." Macoran's voice was soft and compassionate when he continued. "Why did ye not come tell me?"

"He took our only horse. The one we have wandered onto our land or we would have been forced to walk to the village to do the marketing."

"Say the word and I will find yer husband and kill him for deserting ye." Macoran took the empty bucket Jirvel carried, dipped it in the river and let it fill with water. Then he pulled it out and set it down on a flat rock.

Her arms were folded tight and it was all she could do to keep her voice down so Kannak would not hear. "I dinna want ye to kill him, I want yer pledge. Ye have taken everything else from me, but ye will not take Kannak. Ye will let her become a lass and choose her own husband."

"Choose her own husband?"

"If she lived under yer roof ye would let her."

"Be fair, if I let her, the other lassies will want the same."

"I see, 'tis I who must be fair." She closed her eyes and tried to calm down, but her rage only increased. "Ye held me in yer arms and swore ye would never let any harm come to me. Then to cover our sin, ye convinced me to marry a man who never once believed Kannak was his."

"He could not have known for sure."

"Aye, he could."

"How?"

"He did not desire me."

Macoran blinked repeatedly and brought a hand up to rub his brow. "Not even on yer wedding night?"

"Did ye expect him to that night after what happened?"

"I suppose not. But later, when…"

"Not ever. He sought his comfort elsewhere and our marriage was never consummated."

Suddenly unsteady, Macoran had to take a deep breath. "I had not imagined that." He was quiet for a long moment before he spoke again. "I imagined the opposite and wanted to kill Eogan that night and every night since." He tried to take her in his arms but she moved out of his reach. "Jirvel, each time ye came to the village, ye seemed happy and after a while, I convinced myself ye had forgotten our love. But I had not forgotten and seeing ye happy without me nearly did me in."

"Then I pity ye, but not enough to give over my daughter. Tell me now ye will not marry her off to a lad she could never learn to love. 'Tis a fate worse than death."

Macoran tried to gently touch the side of her face, "Am I never to be forgiven?"

She turned her face away, "Ye have a wife, go home to her."

That enraged him and he gritted his teeth. "Ye are not the only one who was forced into a loveless marriage." He took hold of her waist, jerked her to him and wrapped his arms tight around her. "All these years I have thought of nothing but ye. My heart cries out for ye and my arms ache to hold ye. Dinna deny me this once."

As much as she wanted to, she did not yield to his embrace. "Promise ye will not take Kannak."

He drew in another deep breath and slowly let it out. "I see now I owe ye at least that much."

Finally she leaned into him put her arms around his waist, closed her eyes and let herself remember how it once was. Many a year passed and all she had were vague memories of his warmth and his strength. For a while, she let the years dissolve away, but when he tried to kiss her, she pulled back. "We have sinned enough, ye and I."

"I still love ye."

"If ye love me, ye will stay away."

"Ye know I cannae. I must visit every farm when I ride the land."

"Then dinna ride the land so often. Yer nearness be torture for me." Tears started to well up in the rims of her eyes. "Ye stayed away all these years. Please, please dinna make me suffer now." She picked up the pail of water and walked away.

Stefan was not yet old enough to completely understand the love between a man and a woman, but he could not help but pity the man Jirvel left standing alone on the bank of the river even if he did wear Anundi's sword. He looked to be in just as much pain as Stefan felt over losing his father. Perhaps they were the same. Perhaps it is the loss of love that hurts so very much. He watched Macoran gaze aimlessly across the water until at length, the laird walked away.

*

Agnes Macoran might appear to be a frail woman on the outside, but inside she was as strong as the jagged rocks on the shore – and she was filled with wrath. She was painfully thin, a skinny malink longlegs her husband called her when she was out of his presence. Her blond hair was also thin, she had a long hook nose and brown eyes that appeared to be set a little too far apart.

She often walked barefoot along the edge of the ocean, hoping the Vikings would come back. The sun was high in the sky and if she would let herself, she might enjoy watching the steady rhythm of the water rushing in and then withdrawing. But she loved her mystery too much to let any sort of pleasure interfere.

Agnes was the wife of a laird, mistress of an entire clan and she hated every one of them. She hated their red hair, their green eyes, their smiles and especially their laughter. Even her sons reminded her of her unhappiness and to them she gave just a touch more affection than she gave her husband…which was none at all.

She was the youngest daughter of Laird Brodie and it was with him she longed to be. Ripped away from her clan at the age of twenty, she left behind dozens of friends, her mother, her siblings and her beloved father, whom she was convinced favored her above all others.

Macoran tried in the beginning to win Agnes over, and he was civil for the most part even now, but she was consumed with her desire to go home. A spinster she might well have become, but anything would have been better than being so cruelly torn from the people she loved.

Occasionally she contemplated having an adulterous affair so Macoran would set her aside and send her back, but there was not much chance of that even if she were pretty enough to entice a man. Her husband was powerful with all authority of execution and few were willing to cross him.

Every spring Macoran sent his guard with her on the two day journey inland to visit her parents and she stayed until her father insisted she return in the fall. When she was not with child by the third year, he accused her, and rightly so, of not submitting to her husband. There was nothing she would not do to please her father, even that. So she plied her husband with strong drink, enticed him into her bedchamber and the next year she gave birth to twin boys, both with Macoran's awful red hair and green eyes.

That was the end of her wifely duties to her way of thinking and Macoran did not complain. Why should he? Daily he went off on his horse to see that Jirvel woman, whom Agnes was sure he was bedding despite her having a husband of her own. And Agnes was glad of it. Another wife might have been embarrassed by his blatant actions, but she cared not what the Macorans thought of her…or of him.

Yet there had to be a way out of her lifeless marriage so she could go home for good, and the more she thought about it the more only one answer came to mind – Macoran had to die.

Until she found a way to accomplish that, she had two little secret weapons she was more than willing to use to make his life as miserable as he made hers. Macoran named them Searc and Sionn.

*

Kannak was excited about the coming festival and could hardly concentrate on her share of the work during the day not to mention making baskets at night. She waited until Stefan finished sharpening his sword and put it in his sheath. "Perhaps ye would like to learn basket weaving."

"Basket weaving be for lasses and wee bairn."

"Is that so? I say ye *will* not, because ye *can*not."

He got up from the table and hung his sword on a hook on the wall. "Good. I am pleased that be settled. For a moment, I feared another wager coming on. No doubt ye have tired o' losing." Stefan tested the position of the sword to be sure he could draw it easily in the night and then sat back down at the table. "Tonight, 'tis I who will challenge ye."

Jirvel set her basket aside and folded her arms. "I cannae wait to hear it. What be yer challenge?"

"I wager Kannak cannae make a suitable belt from the deer hides."

Kannak suspected a catch somewhere, set her basket down and folded her arms just like her mother's. "How hard could it be?"

"Too hard for ye, I wager. A belt must be strong as well as comely. Shall I show ye or are ye too young still?"

Jirvel was intrigued. "Belts?"

"Aye. Ye said the lads have taken to wearing loose fitting pants and they will need belts. If we can craft them…"

Jirvel's eyes lit up and she didn't let him finish. "If we can craft them well enough, we can make a handsome profit." Jirvel was thrilled. She grabbed her basket, the heather she was using to weave it and handed both to Kannak. "Clear the table," she ordered, and then she went out the door to gather the tanned hides.

Stefan showed them how to carefully scrape the fur away and then cut the deer hide into wide strips they could fold over to make a double thickness. Then he cut thin strips to use for thread. Once that was done, he folded the hide in half lengthwise, cut evenly spaced, slanted slits through both layers in the first section and showed them how to weave the thread through the slits, making the belt stronger as well as decorative. In the next section, he showed them how to make a hidden pocket by cutting the slits in only the top layer and continuing the weave to conceal where the hidden pocket was.

At last, he sat back and enjoyed the delight in their eyes, especially Jirvel's. He felt as though he had given her a precious gift and she deserved it.

As they worked, Jirvel and Kannak asked a hundred questions about his previous life and he told them all about his years growing up with his aunt, uncle and cousins. But he said nothing of the Vikings, the long voyage across the North Sea or the man he had come to call, Commander. It was still too painful. He missed his mother's sister too, but there was nothing he could do about it. As each day passed, he became more and more grateful he had Jirvel and Kannak to fill the void.

*

"But have ye seen a dragon?"

Stefan stopped pulling weeds and looked at her. Her green eyes sparkled with a challenge of some sort and he tried to guess what it was. He knew he was also being goaded into talking about the Vikings, but perhaps just this once. "Nay, wee bairn, but that does not mean they dinna exist. My father believed it, my friend Anundi believed it and so do I."

"And did ye see any sea monsters, bletherskite?"

"Nay, but Anundi did. They have very large mouths and spit water on the ships. Once a sea monster lifted a Viking ship clear out o' the water and dumped it over tossing the lads into the sea."

He looked so sincere when he told it she almost believed him. "But the lads go to sea anyway?"

"Aye, 'tis the way o' the Vikings. What else would they do?"

She thought about that for a moment and then her eyes brightened.

"I wager there are no dragons."

He could see no way for her to win short of going to sea herself, so he considered it. "Wager what?"

"If ye win, I will take ye to see a hidden castle."

"And if ye win?"

"Ye will teach me how to swim."

Stefan frowned, "Ye are not yet strong enough to swim in the river."

"Aye, but I know where there be a loch with warmer water."

"Agreed. Now will ye go get the seed? The time for planting will soon leave us."

They had not seen the horse in days and supposed it was gone for good, but it suddenly broke through the trees and headed straight for them. To keep the stallion out of the garden, both Kannak and Stefan walked toward it. But when they neared, the horse stopped and then backed up.

"What do ye think be wrong with him?" Kannak asked.

Stefan reached out a hand to pat the stallion's nose, but again the horse backed away. Then he caught the reflection in the horse's eye and saw three men standing on the river path behind him. They wore different colored shirts than the Macoran clan and suddenly alarmed, Stefan quickly spun around and drew his sword. "Get behind me, Kannak."

She heard the fear in his voice, instantly obeyed and yelled for her mother.

Jirvel set her bowl on the table and rushed out the door. But as soon as she saw the men she shrieked with delight. "Greagor!" She ran to the one in the middle and threw her arms around his neck. Deliriously happy, she hated to let go of him but at length she stepped back and turned to her daughter. "Do ye remember my brother, Kannak?"

Stefan put his sword away and learned his lesson well. He let himself become distracted, had not been aware of the strangers and it might have been disastrous. He had the horse to thank for bringing that to his attention and this time when he walked to it, the stallion stood still and let him pat his neck. Stefan vowed he would not be so neglectful ever again and started that day to know exactly who and what was around him.

*

Jirvel fixed a banquet fit for a king with vegetables, fresh bread and the smoked salmon she preserved the day before. The men ate hearty and for hours after told stories of the northern clans, which delighted both Stefan and Kannak. Greagor did most of the talking, telling of how he became laird, of great battles, brave men, waterfalls, sparse land, and of the giant living among them.

"Why have ye come," Jirvel asked her brother finally.

"We seek wives. We have not seen a comely lass since ye left us to marry Laird…"

Jirvel quickly interrupted, "Ye flatter me, brother, but we have few unmarried lasses in our clan."

Kannak was incredulous. "Ye came here to marry a laird? Which one?"

"He died, Kannak." Jirvel watched her brother's face and prayed he would not contradict her.

But Kannak would not be so easily put off, "'Tis the first I heard o' it."

Greagor smiled at the niece he had only seen a few times since her birth. "Ye will soon learn a lass keeps many things to herself. Dinna pester yer mother, 'tis plain to see the wound in her heart be not yet healed." He waited to be sure the girl would ask no more questions and then stood up and turned to face his sister. "Is Macoran yet yer laird? Of course he is, I would have heard had he died and from the looks o' things, he has not provided for ye. Yer clothes are old and patched, ye have no sheep to sheer for the wool necessary to make new, the land be unkempt and…"

"My husband be to blame for our condition."

"Aye he be, but so be Macoran. He promised he would see to yer care. 'Tis time I had a talk with…"

Jirvel started to panic. The last thing she wanted was for her brother to confront Macoran. "The fault be mine. I dinna wish to burden our laird."

Greagor knew exactly what she meant. His sister wanted no part of the man who had cast her off at the last moment. "Now that yer husband be gone, come home with us, lass. We will see ye want for nothing."

"I am tempted, but this be my home."

He knew what that meant too. She still loved Macoran and although she could not be his wife, she could not leave him either. Greagor took her in his arms and held his sister tight. "Send the laddie if ye change yer mind and we will come fetch ye."

CHAPTER VII

It was a celebration; a festival of spring not unlike those Stefan had often attended in his homeland, with a multitude of people gathered in the center of the village. Occasionally, men would size him up, but as soon as they realized Stefan was just a boy, none of them said anything about the Viking that got away.

Kannak and Stefan enjoyed the men with painted faces who acted the part of the village idiot. The jokesters walked through the crowd, made funny faces and occasionally danced a comical jig to the music of a flute. Tables held a variety of sweet fruits and breads, ale, mead and wine to complement the plentiful assortment of berries, meats and fish. It was all free for the taking and Stefan ate his fill.

Kannak took him to see the wide mouth of the river, the rafts and the fishing boats, most of which were moored across the river on the Clan Limond side. When they went back to the festival, he too was interested in all the items made by other clan members such as new sheepskin flasks, assorted leather pouches and weapons he would have liked taking home with them. But again he decided showing his wealth would be unwise.

Stefan turned from the tables and began to study the people instead. The Macoran clan had more than its share of elders each of whom looked to be in their early fifties. In his homeland, many did not live that long and no one was quite certain why. A man who married late in life was not likely to see his children grown and it was something to keep in a young man's mind. Even so, Stefan was not the least bit interested in marriage.

*

At the edge of the village, two boys nearing the age of ten were fascinated with a campfire left unattended. First the twins spit on the fire to hear it sizzle, and then they tried to entice a cat to come to them hoping to throw it in the fire. To their chagrin the cat got away. They looked around for other things to throw in the fire, and found little more than sticks and the widow Sarah's favorite marketing basket. Searc, the eldest by only minutes, tossed the basket in and ran. Quickly followed by his brother, Sionn, the two hid behind a cottage and peeked around the corner. No one came and they were not caught. They watched until the basket was consumed, and then exchanged shrugs. Not much excitement in that.

At last Searc had a grand idea. He found a long stick, wrapped a cloth around one end of it, set the cloth on fire and then carried it toward a horse tied to the branch of a tree. He hoped to set the horse's tail on fire, but the terrified horse danced frantically until it managed to pull the reins free and then bolted toward the center of the village.

*

In front of the keep, Macoran and his wife sat in chairs on a raised landing with five steps on either end leading down to the courtyard. From there, he could see everything that was going on and the members of his clan could all see him. Their laird nodded his approval each time a woman brought a taste of this or that for his pleasure, glancing often at Jirvel who seemed intent on examining each of the baskets the other women had made. She was quite good at ignoring him – too good.

It was Macoran who spotted the runaway horse headed into the market place first. People quickly darted out of the way and two of the men tried to catch it, but neither was fast enough. Nor could they understand why the brown mare with a white mane and tail was running for its life.

In disbelief, Macoran stood up. Men began to shout a warning, but the playing of the flute and the noise of the crowd made it impossible to hear and…Jirvel was directly in the horse's path. Panicked, Macoran added his shout to the others and started for the steps.

At the last second Stefan realized what was happening, dove in front of the horse and knocked Jirvel out of the way. He landed on top of her and was certain he hurt her. But he waited until the horse was gone, then quickly rolled off, sat up and turned Jirvel over. The look of shock on her face said it all and an instant later, Macoran scooped her up off the ground and was holding her in his arms.

"I hit her too hard, I knocked the wind out of her," a frantic Stefan said as he scrambled to his feet. The stunned crowd had grown completely silent, each eye held on the woman who was still not breathing.

Macoran leaned her back until her head nearly touched the ground and then jerked her up, "Breathe Jirvel, ye may not leave us, do ye hear me lass?" She did not respond and Macoran was horrified.

Just as worried, Kannak grabbed her mother's arm, "Breathe, mother, please breathe"

He was about to try tipping her back again when at last she blinked her eyes, drew in a huge gulp of air and started to cry. "Dinna weep, ye are safe now," Macoran whispered.

Kannak finally remembered to take a breath of her own and when she saw the worry in her laird's eyes, she tried to reassure him. "Mother always cries when she be frightened."

Standing not far away, Stefan was beside himself, "I am so sorry, Jirvel."

"Sorry? Ye saved her life, laddie. The horse surely would have killed her." Macoran turned his attention back to the woman in his arms. "Are ye hurt, can ye stand?" She nodded, so he lowered her feet to the ground and held on until she got her balance.

Everyone was watching them, even Macoran's wife who still sat in her chair on the landing and Jirvel began to feel ill at ease. She wiggled free of his hand, straightened her frock, brushed the dirt off her long sleeves and smiled at her daughter. "I am fine now." But when she started to curtsey to her laird, a pain shot through her right foot.

She tried to hide her wince, but Macoran was watching her face too closely and took hold of her arm again. He looked around for a chair, spotted one and helped her to it. As soon as she sat down, Macoran knelt down, removed her shoe and felt her ankle for broken bones. "Can ye move it, lass?"

"Well enough to kick *ye*."

He smiled, several of the people laughed and the mood changed back to the festivities of the day. But Macoran was not convinced until she moved her foot up and down and then side to side. He slipped her shoe back on and stood up. Then he turned to Stefan. "She is to rest and I will have a lad see all of ye home safely." He watched Kannak fuss over her mother for a moment, and then he put a fatherly arm around

Stefan's shoulders and began to weave the boy through the crowd toward the landing. "All o' the members o' my clan are precious to me and I am tortured that I did not realize Kannak and her mother were alone. Tell me, what can I do to help them?"

Unsure of how much he should say, Stefan hesitated. "Well…"

Macoran stopped and removed his arm from the boy's shoulders. "Go on, I need to hear it."

"When Kannak's father left he took all the weapons. I worry when I leave them alone to go on the hunt."

Laird Macoran spat on the ground, "That scunner! I will see to it. What else?"

"They have no hooks for fishing. I go after dark when the fish will come to the light and I can spear them. And…they need new clothing."

"Yer a good laddie and ye will be a great lad someday. Tell me, what shall yer reward be for saving Jirvel's life?"

A slow grin crossed Stefan's face, "Yer sword."

Macoran roared with laughter and slapped the boy on the back. "When ye have saved ten lasses, it will be yers. Come, I will have ye meet my wife and children." He stopped, glanced back to see if Jirvel was alright and then leaned just a little closer. "My wife be not so friendly, but pay her no mind. Her father made her marry me and she be unhappy still."

*

For the better part of two hours, Stefan sat beside Laird Macoran on the landing, watched, listened and talked when called upon to do so. Just as Macoran warned, his wife was standoffish and said nothing. She looked incredibly bored but Stefan suspected there was little she did not notice. Laird Macoran's twin sons, Searc and Sionn, were not in the least standoffish. They behaved when they were with their father but once out of his sight, they peeked around the side of a cottage, decided Stefan was the funniest thing they had ever seen, pointed at him and laughed. Soon they scampered away to find more exciting mischief.

Stefan ignored them and went back to watching the festival now that he had a high perch from which to observe. What he enjoyed most was watching Macoran watch Jirvel and then watching her ignore him. It was a sort of game they played and on the few occasions when Jirvel looked at him, Macoran seemed to perk up because of it. Conversely, he stiffened every time another man approached her and there were several over the course of the afternoon.

What fascinated Stefan even more was how much Kannak looked like her father and he wondered how no one else noticed. But then, many in the clans were related in one way or another and most in the Macoran Clan had red hair and green eyes.

*

True to his word, Macoran had a man see them home safely and left them with a sword, two daggers, a fishing spear and small iron fishing hooks. As soon as they were home and Jirvel was comfortable in her bed with her foot propped up to help the swelling, both she and Kannak would not rest until they knew every word he and Macoran exchanged.

Kannak sat on the bed next to her mother and was especially worried, "Did he ask about yer clan in the north?"

"Aye," was all Stefan was willing to say.

She lowered her head and glared at him through the top of her eyes. "Are ye not to tell us?"

"If ye must know, I told o' a very tall man in the north who is slow o' wit, a plentiful waterfall and land with few trees. I may have mentioned I prefer trees."

"And what else?" asked Kannak.

He winked at Jirvel and headed for the doorway. "I told him the lasses were not as beautiful in the north as they are here." With that, he walked out of the bedchamber, went to the front door and checked to be sure it was bolted. Then he climbed into bed and covered himself. They were still giggling when he fell into a peaceful sleep.

*

Two days later, Macoran had a horse and a good size collection of woven cloths delivered including linen for undergarments. It was just in time for Stefan's long pants would be too short soon.

Instead of being a tall, sleek, black horse, this one was mostly white with one large brown spot on its rump. It was also short and stocky with an ample width fit for hard work and long hours of travel. Until Stefan got bigger, all three could comfortably ride this horse together which was a good thing because the stallion disappeared again.

Kannak and Stefan were thrilled with the new horse...Jirvel was suspicious. The word 'bribery' came to mind. But as time passed and nothing was asked of her or Kannak, Jirvel began to take to the mare herself, riding her after the day's work was done, grooming her and making sure she would come when Jirvel whistled. It was yet another measure of comfort and safety she was happy to have. Once, the mare came to the door of the cottage and pushed it open with its head as though it was looking for Jirvel. For days, Stefan and Kannak could not stop laughing about it.

*

The early days of spring turned into the long days of summer and they had sunlight for all but a few hours a night. With the planting finished, Stefan fixed things in the cottage and the shed when it was raining, and clearing heather from more land when it was not. He tended the garden, hunted and fished while Jirvel and Kannak made new clothing for them all.

If only he knew how to make shoes. At length, he decided to tear his old pair apart to make a pattern, cut new, larger pieces from a deer hide and make his own. They were not the best by any means, but they would do. Kannak laughed at him until he challenged her to make a better pair. That was the end of her laughter on that subject.

Then one day, after the women returned from bartering the belts they made, Jirvel produced a new pair made by the Macoran cobbler. The cobbler used his old, torn apart pair to make the patterns, they fit perfectly with a little room to grow and he was so pleased, he hugged her.

CHAPTER VIII

They went to see about it at the same time for the sad whimper of a dog was a sure sign it was hurt. But when Stefan finally found it, it was not a dog but a gray wolf. Just as he parted the bushes and saw the animal lying on its side hopelessly tangled up in twine, bushes on the other side of the wolf parted and he was face to face with a boy not much younger than he.

Stefan nodded and then pulled out his dagger, "I say we cut it free."

"I say we kill it," the boy said. "Many's the lamb who will not be sorry to be shed o' that one."

"This wolf? This precise wolf? Have ye any proof?"

"'Tis a wolf, what more proof are ye need'n?"

The animal's eyes were wide with fright and Stefan felt sorry for it. "Even a wolf has the right to survive any way it can and this one has cubs somewhere."

"Aye but…"

"We kill lambs for food too, should we be put to death?"

There was little the other laddie could say, though he did wrinkle his brow. "If I help ye free it, do ye pledge not to tell my father?"

"I do."

The boy knelt down, struggled for a moment to get a firm hold on the wolf's mouth to clamp it shut and then held its front paws while

Stefan carefully cut the twine away. They stared at each other, then when the boy nodded, both he and Stefan let go and quickly moved away. The scared wolf scrambled to its feet and darted through the bushes toward the river. Then it stopped and looked back at them for a long moment.

"Ye are welcome," said Stefan. With that, the animal ran down the river bank and out of sight.

"I am Diarmad from Clan Macoran."

"I am Stefan…"

"I know, we have all heard. Is it true there be a giant in the north that be slow o' wit?"

"Aye." Stefan had a feeling he was about to get trapped in his lie and decided to head home.

But Diarmad quickly caught up. "When ye go north again, may I go with ye? I would see this giant."

So would I, Stefan thought. "'Twill be a long time afore I go back."

Diarmad was disappointed. "But when ye do, will ye take me?"

Stefan stopped and looked at his new friend. Already he was much taller than Diarmad who had the famous light skin and red hair of the Macorans. Nevertheless, he had blue eyes instead of green and a warm smile. Stefan hesitated to agree to take him north, but decided a lot could happen before then and he probably would not be held to his promise. "Aye."

"Macoran told us all about ye, 'er I should say he told some and they spread it around. Gossip be our favorite diversion."

"'Tis the same where I come from. Where do ye live?"

“Just beyond the trees. We know Jirvel’s husband cast her off. Two other men went with him. Does she know where they have gone? Macoran would surely like to know, he be none too pleased about it.”

“She does not and she is well rid o’ her husband from what I can see.”

“Everyone says he was not inclined to marry her just as she was not inclined to marry him, but they married just the same. Her husband loved another, they say.”

Stefan was intrigued. “Why do they say that?”

“Because the lass he wanted to marry…and who wanted to marry him…killed herself the day he married Jirvel.”

Stefan quickly crossed himself. Then he found a large rock and sat down. “Does Jirvel know?”

“Aye, the lass hung herself from a branch of that tree next to Jirvel’s cottage and it was Jirvel who found her.”

Stefan could think of nothing worse and closed his eyes. He liked Jirvel and could only imagine how much pain it caused her. “Tell me, if neither wanted it, why did Eogan marry Jirvel?”

“That, no one knows for sure but greed be the suspect. ‘Tis said Eogan wanted the land and the only way Macoran would grant it, was if he married Jirvel. ‘Tis said Eogan planned to marry her, accuse her of adultery, set her aside and then marry the lass he loved. That way he could have both his preferred lass and the land.”

“But the lass he loved did not know o’ his plan.”

“It would seem not. Are ye the missing Viking?”

Stefan rolled his eyes. “They have not yet found him?” He quickly searched his mind for something the boy could spread around that would end the suspicion. "As yer well aware, there are many Vikings in the north. I have heard of two who swam a great distance to get to a longship. Perhaps he…"

Diarmad's eyes grew wide and he quickly found a rock opposite Stefan to sit on. "In these cold waters?"

"Aye, they are very strong lads."

"'Tis possible, I suppose. We did not see a lad in the water, but we were not looking for one either."

"'Tis not like the Vikings to leave a lad behind. Perhaps they came back in the night to get him."

"That be possible too."

He should ask about the battle. Any other laddie who had not been there would, but Stefan could not stand to hear it. "Have ye any brothers and sisters?"

Diarmad grinned. "If ye've a need for a sister, I would be happy to give over five or six. There are seven, all told, but I like the eldest. Her name be Andrina and ye will like her too. She has her wits about her."

"No brothers?"

"Two, both older and set to take wives soon. I dread the day they are gone and I am alone with all those…lassies."

"And yer parents?"

"Mother gave up the ghost two years hence and father has asked for Jirvel."

He remembered Macoran saying two men had asked for her and Diarmad's father must be one of them. "She be married still."

"Aye, but when the priest comes after the harvest to collect the tithe, father hopes to convince him to set her marriage aside."

"He can do that? Yer father, I mean?"

"Our priest is not an unreasonable man. He knows 'tis impossible for a lass to manage alone. Plus…"

"What?"

"Father will offer an extra tithe for it."

"And if Jirvel refuses to marry him?"

Diarmad looked shocked, "Lasses are not allowed to refuse. Once Macoran agrees, she be betrothed."

Stefan spotted a small round stone in the dirt, leaned over and picked it up. Long ago his father taught him how to play a game with round rocks and he was starting a collection for the son he would have some day. "I dinna see how forcing a lass to marry be o' benefit to the husband. I want a wife who loves me."

"I confess not all marriages are blissful, but father says a lass learns to love her husband later. He says most are grateful just to have a husband."

"I dinna want a grateful wife, I want one who will be happy to see me when I come home, will be proud to stand by my side and who wants my children. I will settle for nothing less."

Diarmad scratched the side of his head. "Let a lass choose, ye mean? 'Tis unheard of."

"'Tis *not* unheard of. A lass wants to be truly in love just like most lads. I would want that kind of love for Jirvel and Kannak." He quickly stood up and headed back to the cottage. Suddenly he did not like Diarmad's father.

"Wait, are ye saying Jirvel would refuse to marry my father even if Macoran proclaimed it?"

Stefan slowed and let Diarmad catch up. "Would ye like seeing yer Andrina married to a lad she did not love just because yer laird proclaimed it?"

"She would learn to love him."

"Ye cannae truly believe that. Suppose he be a drunkard like Eogan or slothful or even cruel to her. How then is she supposed to learn to love him?" He had said too much for the boy looked in complete misery. "Dinna fret, when she be old enough to marry, we will find a way to prevent the wrong lad from taking her."

"She be old enough now. She be fourteen."

"Has a lad asked for her?"

"Not yet, but father says they will soon. What can we do?"

"I can do little, but ye have an advantage. Ye know the lads and can judge which will be good to her. Perhaps ye might arrange for the lad o' yer choosing and yer sister to be together somehow. But see that he be not old for her sake."

"I will think on it. Perhaps ye might want her."

"I dinna want a wife nor do I have anything to offer one."

Diarmad was disappointed but it passed quickly. "Will ye help me? Perhaps tomorrow we could go to the village and have a look see at the lads."

"I have much to do here, but I will ask Jirvel. Tell me, did ye come for a particular reason?"

"Oh, I near forgot. Father sent me to see if ye want the cow bred. 'Tis our bull what does it normally."

"Come to the cottage and we will ask Jirvel."

"Ask a lass?"

"'Tis her cow."

"Nay, 'tis Macoran's cow." Diarmad suddenly grinned. "'Tis a worthy cause to go to the village tomorrow and ask Macoran. Do ye agree?"

Stefan returned his smile. "A worthy cause indeed."

*

Because of her husband's drunkenness, Jirvel and Kannak had little social life except for the occasional visit to the village, and Jirvel was surprised when a knock at the door produced the widower Ronan from the land next to hers and his seven daughters. He was not an unpleasant looking man, but he was much older and almost shorter than Jirvel.

The girls ranged in age from five to fourteen and all began to talk at once. "We have come to help," said the eldest." Andrina was a pretty girl whom often wished she and Kannak could be friends. She suspected Eagan forbid it in the past, but now that he was gone, she was hopeful.

"We are good at planting and we have finished ours," another of the girls proudly announced. "And we noticed…could not help but notice, yer chickens need a pen to keep them safe. We can put up three walls, if'n we use the back o' yer shed for the fourth. We make excellent walls and yer land has plenty o' rocks."

The smallest child pushed her way through the others, came in the door, raised her arms to Jirvel and waited for her to pick her up. "I am Suria. We seen three berry bad wolves. I are a feared o' 'em, are ye?"

"Nay, we have Stefan to protect us." She smiled at the child's father and since there were so many of them, decided to carry the little one outside to talk. Kannak was thrilled and quickly walked out to stand beside Andrina.

But Stefan was not so pleased. While they needed the help and badly, he did not like the way Ronan looked at Jirvel and he had not forgotten what Diarmad said the day before about bribing the priest so she would be free to marry. Nevertheless, he politely greeted the girls and then spotted Diarmad standing by a tree holding the reins of two horses. He preferred to ride their horse but the mare would not come to him. He needed Jirvel to whistle and she was busy talking.

Jirvel set the child down and curtsied to Ronan as a sign of respect even though it was not required for any man save their laird. "Ye are very kind to help us." She meant it too. They only had two chickens left and with no pen, Jirvel had to rely on her nightly prayer to keep them safe.

"Ye may not be so happy once ye see what these can eat o' a noon meal. Just in case, I brought two loaves o' bread." He handed her a cloth sack. "If that be not enough, I can send the laddies for…"

"'Tis more than enough."

Ronan nodded and went to his horse. "Best ye take our other horse for yer ride into the village, Stefan, and leave the mare in case the lassies need to come get us for some reason." He mounted and then rode his horse out of the courtyard and turned down the path.

But the other horse Diarmad held the reins to had a saddle and Stefan much preferred to ride bare back. Before he even asked, Jirvel whistled and it wasn't long until the mare came running. He bridled her, mounted and then turned to the woman he was beginning to think of more as a mother than just a good friend. "We will not tarry long."

When he looked, Kannak and Andrina were whispering, looking at him and giggling. Stefan rolled his eyes.

"Enjoy yer day, Stefan. Perhaps ye should see more o' our land and meet more o' the people. We will be well." She saw the look of worry in his eyes and sought to comfort him further. "Ye forget, we have weapons now and we know how to use them. Be gone with ye two."

He still hesitated, but finally led the way up the same path Ronan took. After a time and when the path was wide enough, Diarmad moved his horse up beside Stefan's. "There be a certain lad we might consider for Andrina. His name be Blair and he has already had a wife, but she died six months ago with the birth o' her first. A lass in the village cares for her bairn, but Blair visits often. To my way o' thinking, only a good lad would do that."

"I agree." He let Diarmad take the lead and as they rode past farm after farm, Diarmad had this and that to say about each, mostly good things but occasionally he was critical of the man for his farming skills. It appeared farming skills were far more important to Diarmad than the man's care of his wife and children, but Stefan kept his thoughts to himself.

When they came to a place in the path that was flooded, Diarmad halted his horse. "Searc and Sionn have been here, I see." He turned his horse off the path, found the creek and just as he thought, rocks and mud had been piled in the creek to force the water onto the path.

"Why do ye suspect Macoran's sons o' this?" Stefan dismounted and began to move the rocks out of the creek.

"Who else would do it? They are a pest and blight on us all. The laddies particularly like to cause the widow Sarah's discomfort. She has a sharp voice when she be riled and they do all they can to get her so. Once they put eggs in her chair and she neglected to look before she sat. Her screeching was so loud, half the Limonds came to the river to see if they were needed."

"And Macoran does nothing to stop his sons?"

"They are well trained to keep out o' sight and not get caught."

"Trained by whom?"

"Mistress Agnes, 'tis said, though none have the proof. If they did, they would tell Macoran. God help us all when those two are grown. We will no doubt be tempted to tell the Vikings where to find them." Diarmad joined his laughter to Stefan's, watched him get back on his horse and then led the way back to the path. "The twins particularly like fire and more than once a lad or lass has pulled them away from one just in time. At least we have one saving grace."

"What might that be?"

"In the spring, Macoran sends them off with their mother to the Brodie's. 'Tis the most blessed time o' the year for us all."

CHAPTER IX

Kannak could not have been happier. Andrina was full of gossip and while the younger girls went off to gather heather to mix with the river clay her mother went to fetch, the older girls began to fill baskets with rocks.

"He be handsome enough, I suppose," said Kannak. "But Stefan grows more awkward by the moment. Mother says he be growing and all boys become ungainly when they dinna realize their size."

"'Tis true, my brothers are the same."

"When do they grow out o' it? I sometimes fear Stefan will trample me."

"When they stop growing. Awkward or not, Stefan be almost as handsome as…"

Kannak put a rock in her basket and then tested the weight to see if it was getting too heavy. "As who?"

"I best not say."

"Why not? I would not tell even if I had other friends."

"Do ye pledge it?"

"Of course." She added two more rocks and decided it was heavy enough.

Andrina leaned a little closer. "William be the most princely lad I have ever seen."

"William? The William who lives just east o' us?" She waited for

Andrina to lift her basket and together they carried them back to where Jirvel was digging a hole in which to mix the clay with water. Already the younger girls had gathered a full basket of heather to mix in the mortar. They dumped the rocks in a pile and went back.

"Do ye know him, William I mean?" asked Andrina.

"Not well, but I have seen him often. He seems pleasant enough."

"I think so too. I have not yet had occasion to talk with him much. Come to think o' it, I have not talked to him at all."

"Why not?"

"I dinna know precisely. It would help if he was our direct neighbor, but ye live between us, ye see. I did catch him looking at me during the festival, but he did not approach." Andrina tossed several more rocks in her basket and then stood up to stretch her back.

"Is that how it be done? The lad approaches the lass he hopes to marry?"

"How else is he to know if she has a soft enough voice or if she smells. A lad does not like a lass who smells, ye know."

Kannak had never thought of that reason to keep clean and decided she would take more care of her personal grooming in the future, just in case Jirvel ever let her marry, which she doubted would be any time soon…if ever. "What do they talk about when a lad approaches?"

Andrina giggled. "I have only been approached once. It was Friseal and he asked if I was a good cook. I did not like him, so I shook my head and he went away. My father glared at me for the rest o' the day."

"Yer father wishes ye to marry?"

"He wishes us all to marry and quickly, save the brothers. He has too many mouths to feed and no wife. But ye dinna see my meaning."

"Meaning o' what?"

"Macoran dinna let a lass choose, but if she be very, very wise, she can do the choosing anyway. All she need do is be pleasing to the lad she wants and…"

"Addlebrained to the one she dinna want?"

"Or worse if need be. She might laugh too loud or too often, whisper so he cannae hear her, or I dinna know…there must be many ways to discourage him."

*

It was a beautiful glen that marked the last of the Macoran land and at the end was a vast holding filled with sheep, cattle and horses. A couple of Macoran guards sat their horses at the edge of the land and kept watch for strangers and visitors. The dirt road was wide enough for a cart and the large cottage was surrounded by flowers. "He sees to all this by himself?" Stefan asked.

"Macoran sends lads to help when 'tis needed, but mostly Blair cares for it himself. I would like to see Andrina living in such a fine home. Since our mother passed, she has carried a heavy load. Come, we will meet him and ye can help me decide."

They spent an hour with Blair, but it was apparent he still mourned his wife and was not ready to have another. Even so, Stefan had another new friend and he liked the man very much. Blair had a love for animals and children, the same as Stefan.

On the way back, they next visited Fergus. He was unmarried and he too kept his place well cared for growing wheat and oats mostly. But his cottage was smaller than Jirvel's and when Diarmad suggested he build a new one, Fergus was offended. The boys quickly crossed him off their list as too quick to anger.

There were other farms, but those men were married and as they rode the path, Diarmad and Stefan simply nodded and continued on. On the village side of Jirvel's land lived William and Colin whom they visited respectively. They too were pleasant and Stefan could not find fault with either of them. Both were young, hardworking, not taken to drink and friendly. How would they ever choose? It appeared matchmaking was not as easy as they supposed. One thing was stuck in Stefan's mind and it galled him – why was Jirvel's land so run down compared to the others? Did no one care to help all these years, even her neighbors?

*

As soon as Macoran spotted Stefan riding into the village he grew concerned. Hiding it well, he stood on the landing with his hands clasped behind his back and waited until the young boys approached. "Good day to ye, laddies." He watched them nod and then had to know, "Is something amiss?"

"We have come to ask if ye want Jirvel's cow bred," Diarmad blurted out.

"'Tis Jirvel's cow, ask her."

"Ask a lass?"

"Ah, I see yer meaning. Let me say this then. I cannae be at hand always and I trust Stefan to do the right thing. If he happens to seek Jirvel's advice on a matter or two, so be it."

Diarmad found it very perplexing. Never had he heard of asking a lass's advice on a matter such as this. But if he suspected something, he held his words. "So be it."

"Have ye eaten?" When both shook their heads, he smiled. "Nor have I. Perhaps ye might share a bite with me and tell me all the news."

Diarmad was excited. Until now, he believed he was not yet old enough to be invited inside and especially not for a meal. He dismounted, let another man take his horse away as though he was an honored guest and followed Stefan up the stairs.

The two-story home of Laird Macoran was spacious and clean. It had a kitchen in the back, a stone staircase, a balcony leading to four bedchambers and a large great hall that took up most of the bottom floor. With a stone hearth at one end, the great hall was well furnished and held a polished long table and several high backed chairs.

A great hall was often a place to show off the clan's wealth and if not, the hunting or battle skills of their laird. As soon as he was inside, Stefan spotted an array of confiscated Viking weapons and at first pretended not to notice.

But Diarmad was entranced and slowly walked down the wall examining each article, so Stefan felt he should as well. He hoped he would not recognïze any of them but the latest addition to the collection was his father's shield. It was all he could do not to gasp, but he held his face stoic and swore he would have that back someday. At least his father's sword was not among the prizes. The old ways of the Vikings demanded a man's sword be buried with him to take into the next life.

Diarmad came across a weathered rod with several leather strips attached to it, "What be this, Laird Macoran?"

"'Tis a whip used for flogging by the Romans. Blair found that when he dug his fruit cellar. I dinna believe the Romans made it this far into Scotland, but there's the proof. Wretched looking thing, is it not?"

Stefan expected Macoran's wife and sons to join them, but they were nowhere in sight. "Is yer wife unwell?"

"Nay, she prefers to keep to her bedchamber." He glanced up at a partially closed bedchamber door and frowned. "Take no offense, laddies. 'Tis me she hates."

Macoran motioned for each to sit on opposite sides of the table and then sat down at the head. He patiently waited for the servers to bring more food and extra bowls before he spoke again. "As I recall Diarmad, ye have not been in my company since ye got caught throwing rocks at…"

"Rosa," Diarmad put in. "I recollect it as though it were yesterday. Ye tanned my backside and then my father burned a hole clean through it when he got me home."

Macoran laughed. "Ye've not thrown a rock since, I venture to guess."

"I have not even skipped a pebble across the river since that day."

Again Macoran laughed, "And will ye warm yer son's backside when he does it?"

"Not if he throws it at Rosa, she deserved it."

"How so?"

"She called my mother a bletherskite."

At that, Stefan could not help but smile. "It seems to be a favorite word among the Macorans. Kannak calls me that when she be put out."

Macoran filled a bowl with mutton stew and handed it to Stefan. "Are yer families well?" He filled another for Diarmad and a bowl for himself.

The boys both answered and told of their ride, the visits and the places they had seen. Macoran noticed all the men they visited were unmarried and wondered why, but he let them finish eating before he asked, “Are the two o’ ye thinking o’ taking wives?”

Stefan nearly choked on his last bite of stew. “I dinna want a wife.”

But Diarmad was far more serious. “At what age do ye recommend marriage, Laird Macoran?”

“There be no particular age, but a lad must be able to care for a wife and the children she will bear afore I give my permission. Why did ye not bring Kannak with ye, Stefan?”

“She builds a wall, which reminds me we should get back to help.”

“My father took all his daughters to Jirvel,” Diarmad added. “He thought she might as well get to know them. Of course it be to help build a pen for the chickens as well.” He saw the look of displeasure on Macoran’s face and caught his breath. “Did I talk out o’ turn? My father said he already asked for Jirvel.”

Macoran dared not let his jealousy be exposed particularly since he knew his wife was listening, as she always was. “Nay, laddie, ye did not talk out o’ turn. I was just surprised yer father would take such a bold step. I have not yet given my permission. He be not the only lad who has asked for her.”

“Oh, I see. I dinna believe my father knows that. But he was the first and I have heard ye give yer favors to the first.”

“They say that, do they? I suppose they are right, but not by design. I know ye will find this hard to believe, but I do try to give a lass to a lad who be deserving o’ her. It be not as easy as ye may think. If I choose wrong, the other lad will hate me and when I need him to fight, he will be o' no use to me."

Stefan could not help himself, "I have heard that a lass has no say in the matter."

Macoran stared at Stefan a little longer than he might have otherwise. "Do lasses in the north do the choosing?"

"In some places." Again fearing he was about to get caught in his lies, Stefan quickly continued. "If there be love, sometimes an exception be made."

"Ah love. When I know about it I take it under advisement too. Most men think they are in love when they ask for a lass, but a lass can learn to love her husband no matter who I choose for her."

Stefan thought to argue the point but was certain it would take more than one afternoon to convince Macoran otherwise, and he did not have that kind of time. "We should get back. I worry about leaving Jirvel and Kannak alone."

"If that be the case, yer free to leave." Macoran watched the young men walk out the door and then mumbled, "Love…love will be the death o' us all."

*

Half the wall was finished, the neighbor girls agreed to come back the next day and the three in Jirvel's little family were almost too exhausted to talk during their evening meal. But if they were to be a real family, which Stefan sorely wanted to be a part of, there could be no secrets between them. "Diarmad says the lads will ask for Andrina soon and I am curious; why do the Scots not let the lass have a say in matters of marriage?"

"'Tis because they are daft," Jirvel scoffed. "I have yet to know a lass, forced to take a husband she does not want, who be happy in her marriage."

"But Macoran claims a lass will learn to love her husband no matter who she be matched with."

"Aye, that be what he claims and that be what the lads want him to believe. What lad will admit he cannae make his wife happy?"

"But do the lasses not tell Macoran?"

"'Twould do no good. He would just pat their hands and tell them to give it more time."

"Andrina says a wise lass can out think Macoran." Kannak had their full attention and savored the moment by taking a sip of water and then slowly setting her goblet down. "I am not to tell, but she prefers William and wants no other, not even ye, Stefan."

Jirvel grinned and Stefan rolled his eyes. "I am overjoyed to hear that," he said. "Diarmad and I have discussed it and he wants his sister to marry for love. But suppose another lad asks afore William? Macoran will likely give her to the first."

For a long moment, each of them was lost in thought. Then Jirvel spoke up. "It would serve Macoran right if we did the matchmaking for a change. Tomorrow when the girls return, Stefan will ride to William's cottage and ask him to come help with something."

"Help with what?"

"We will have to think o' something."

"But we cannae tell Andrina what we are up to," said Kannak. Suddenly realizing she had just given Stefan something to hold over her head, she turned her glare on him.

"What did I do?"

"Take a pledge not to tell."

"Ye need a pledge over such a thing as this? Ye dinna trust me, wee bairn?"

"I would be daft to trust a bletherskite?"

"Then ye have my pledge this once, but in the future I will only give it on more important matters. Time for bed, wee bairn."

Kannak would have ignored him, but she was tired enough to go anyway. She got up, put her bowl and goblet in the washing bucket and went off to bed. "Wee bairn indeed." She let the curtain down and disappeared behind it.

Stefan grinned, put a hand on Jirvel's arm to get her attention and whispered, "Ronan has asked Macoran for ye. He was the first and thinks he has ye."

Jirvel took an exhausted breath and let it out. "Thank God I am married."

"He hopes to bribe the priest to set yer marriage aside."

She abruptly caught her breath. "Has Macoran given his permission?"

"He said not and he also reminded Diarmad another has asked for ye as well. Perhaps…"

Kannak shouted from her bedchamber, "What be all the whispering?"

"We hope to annoy ye so ye cannae sleep." Stefan shot back.

"Well 'tis working."

Jirvel smiled, lowered her voice even more and leaned closer, "Perhaps what?"

"Perhaps ye might not smile so sweetly at him tomorrow."

"Perhaps I should spit in his face, ye mean." She brought both hands up and rubbed her temples. "What am I to do?"

"I dinna know."

*

The neighbor girls came early and this time without Diarmad. Just as they had the day before, they took to their tasks of gathering the materials needed to finish the wall. They tried, but neither Jirvel, Kannak nor Stefan could think of a reason to ask for William's help. Just before the noon meal, a reason none of them could have imagined presented itself.

Suria went missing.

The five-year-old was there one moment and gone the next. Jirvel was the first to notice her missing and shouted, "Where might Suria be?" Everyone stopped what they were doing at the same time and looked around.

Several yards away, Andrina cupped her hands and shouted, "She be not lost, Jirvel. She likes to catch butterflies, but she knows not to go far. We will find her."

"I pray yer right," Jirvel whispered. She put down her mixing stick and started to head for the river.

But Stefan stopped her. "I will go to the river. Send the older girls that way." He pointed east toward William's land. "Take the others and search the woods. We will find her."

Soon the voices of nine people filled the air, "Suria!"

Kannak was beside herself with worry, but while Andrina was concerned, she was not in a panic. "We might see William," she whispered between shouts for her sister. "He is so handsome." The closer she got to his cottage, the louder she shouted. "Suria!"

But time drew on, the child was not found and by the time William came through the thick trees on his horse, tears were in Andrina's eyes. "The fault be mine," she sobbed. "I am the one charged with watching her, but I let myself get diverted."

He got down off his horse and put a hand on her shoulder. "Dinna fret yerself so, I will help ye find her."

"Truly?"

He grinned. "I'd not lie at a time like this."

She realized her mistake and tried to smile.

"Did ye see which way she went?"

"Nay. Stefan went to the river and Jirvel and the girls are searching the trees."

"Good. Keep looking here and I will search toward the river also." He did not say it, but William was worried. The currents in the river were swift and more than one child had gotten swept away in it.

*

Stefan was terrified. He could not find the child on the shore nor in the water. But then, if she fell into the water it surely would have washed her away by now. Suddenly, he spotted the gray wolf. It was just standing on the bank watching him and as soon as their eyes met, the wolf took off. But then it stopped and looked back as though it wanted him to follow.

"Suria," he shouted. He paused to listen, heard nothing and then decided to follow the wolf up the river bank. When it got too far ahead, the wolf again stopped and looked back, so Stefan quickened his pace. He had heard of dogs leading someone to the lost, but never a wolf.

"Suria!" he paused, listened and thought he heard a whimper coming from somewhere ahead. He started to run as did the wolf, keeping safely out of Stefan's reach until it stopped near some bushes. "Suria!"

"I am caught."

He was so happy to hear her, he finally allowed himself to breathe. "Where are ye, lassie?"

"Here."

Stefan stepped through the bushes, spotted the top of her head and leaned down to pick her up. But just as she said, her skirt was caught in the bushes and she couldn't pull herself free. Tears were streaming down her cheeks, but she found her voice enough to whisper, "I seed a wolf."

"I saw it too, but it dinna hurt ye. 'Tis a good wolf."

"A good wolf?" As soon as he got her skirt free, she wrapped her little arms around his neck and let him lift her up.

"I must tell the others yer safe." He put two fingers to his mouth and whistled. He could hear shouts in the distance, smiled and started back. The wolf was gone, but to his amazement, Jirvel's horse came running. Stefan laughed, set the child on the horse and swung up behind her. By the time he got the two of them back to the cottage, all six girls, Jirvel, Kannak…and William were waiting.

Andrina ran to the horse, pulled Suria down and kissed her face repeatedly. "Ye must not wander off like that. Ye scared us witless."

"I tore my skirt."

Andrina smiled to comfort her worried little sister. "We will mend it. Now promise ye will not wander off again and I will let ye down."

"I promise. I followed a rabbit, hop, hop, hop … and," she quickly drew in a sharp breath. "A wolf found me, but 'tis a good wolf. It dinna hurt me."

"A good wolf, be it?" William asked.

At last Andrina remembered William was there and returned his smile. "Thank ye for helping us."

"Yer welcome."

He seemed not to want to leave and Stefan noticed. "Might we get yer advice on our wall? I confess I have never built one and I dinna know if it will hold." He hoped Jirvel would not be offended and when he looked, she gave him a slight nod.

"I would be happy to take a look." William turned once more to Andrina, nodded and then followed Stefan toward the wall.

When the girls started to giggle, Jirvel intentionally interrupted. "Back to work everyone. Suria, yer staying with me afore yer father has my head." She grabbed the little girl's hand and followed the men toward the wall.

CHAPTER X

This time when Ronan came to get his daughters, Jirvel was inside the cottage and did not come out to thank him. All seven of his daughters tried to explain what happened to Suria at once and he seemed to be able to hear them all. Relieved that she was alright, he picked her up and hugged her. Then he glanced at Jirvel's cottage to see if she had witnessed his tender display. She had not. "Is yer mother unwell?" he asked Kannak.

"Nay, she be well." Stefan answered for her. He neglected to elaborate on Jirvel's excuse for not being neighborly. Instead, he handed Ronan the empty bread sack. "The wall be nearly finished but we would appreciate Diarmad and Andrina's help again tomorrow."

"And not the others?"

Stefan paused as if trying to find a delicate way to say it and then leaned closer, "Lassies take a great deal more care than laddies, do ye agree?"

Ronan rolled his eyes. "Ye cannae know until ye have seven." He thought about it for a moment. "Very well, ye may have Andrina in the morning, but Diarmad cannae come until after the noon meal."

"Thank ye." It would be perfect, Stefan thought. William was coming to help too and Diarmad need not be where he might interfere. Stefan accepted another hug from Suria for saving her, helped the girls mount their horses and watched them ride away.

*

While Kannak went to do the evening milking, Stefan went inside and took the long bow down off the hook on the wall. He thought the string was a little too loose the last time he used it and wanted to restring it. “Slighting Ronan this once will not be enough.”

Jirvel finished cutting a potato into sections and then laid her knife down. “Perhaps ye might tell him I prefer another.”

“Which other?”

“I dinna know. I can think o’ no lad I fancy.”

“If we do that, Ronan may hasten his plan and go see the priest directly instead o’ waiting for him to collect the tithe after the harvest.”

“Perhaps we should go north after all. I dinna want another husband. One bitter lad be enough for any lass and I suspect Ronan wants this land and the cottage for one o’ his sons far more than he wants me.”

“If only ye had something to threaten Macoran with. Perhaps then he would discourage all the lads who want ye.”

It was almost as if he knew something and Jirvel studied Stefan’s eyes for a moment. Then she dismissed her suspicions and lowered her gaze. “Perhaps I do have something that might persuade him.” She lightly kissed Stefan on the cheek and went back to her potatoes. “Ye are a good son and I could wish for none better.”

Stefan’s heart leapt for joy at her words. Finally he was assured he had a family again and he refused to give this one up. He was not even willing to give up the pesky wee bairn though he would never tell Kannak that.

*

When William and Andrina arrived the next morning, Jirvel was ready to play matchmaker. She handed Andrina two empty pails. "Can ye manage? Will the water be too heavy? Perhaps ye should just fill each half…"

"I will help her," William offered. If he suspected being set up, he did not let on and the two of them walked happily down the path toward the river. Jirvel smiled, Kannak smiled and Stefan grinned. Macoran would not have a hand in this match if the three of them had anything to say about it.

Jirvel mixed the clay, water and heather together in the small pit. Kannak and Andrina went to gather more rocks while the men stacked the stones in two parallel rows and filled the space between them with the mortar to make the third and final wall. It was hard work and Jirvel encouraged the girls to fetch plenty of drinking water. Each time Andrina offered her flask to William, she couldn't help but smile. Nor could William manage to keep his eyes off of her.

When Stefan went off for his comfort and the girls were gathering more rocks, Jirvel became a bit more emboldened. "'Tis it me or 'tis there love in the air?"

With hopeful eyes, William stopped his work and looked at her. "Do ye think so? I mean do ye think Andrina prefers me?"

Jirvel rolled her eyes. "If ye dinna see it in her eyes, yer brain has addled. Ye best ask Macoran for her and quickly afore someone else gets to him."

"I am not worried."

"Why not?"

"I asked for her six months ago, only it has taken this long for her to notice me. I dinna want a wife who does not prefer me."

"If that be the case, I will send her to fetch more water and if yer wise, ye will follow and ask her if she will agree to marry ye."

"But if she says nay…"

"She will not disappoint ye. She preferred ye long afore now."

His eyes instantly lit up and he turned his attention back to laying the rocks. The wall was only three feet high and nearly finished with a wide enough gap in the side for a gate. It might not keep a hungry wolf or red fox out completely, but it would keep the chickens in.

Jirvel smiled, noticed the girls were coming and went back to work. "Love…'tis the only thing in life worth the wait."

*

William and Andrina were married the week after, in the village for all to see and Kannak, her new best friend, attended her while Jirvel pleaded a headache so she could avoid Ronan. After the ceremony and the feast, William carried his beloved off on his horse and took her to his cottage.

It was not the only thing worth celebrating and not long after the newlyweds were last seen, Macoran's guard gathered in front of the keep, loaded Mistress Macoran, her sons and her things on horses and escorted them out of the village to begin the two days of travel to the Brodie hold. The clan wanted to shout for joy, but they held their tongues out of respect for their adored laird. Even so, there was a great deal of gladness among them and especially in the happy eyes and voice of the widow Sarah.

A short time later, Macoran mounted his horse and Stefan was certain he had gone to see Jirvel, so he lingered, talking to Blair and

Fergus until Kannak started to glare at him. Still, he wanted to give Jirvel time to get a promise from Macoran not to betroth her.

*

Somehow Jirvel suspected Macoran would come and even brushed her auburn hair a second time before she loosely braided it and let it hang down the middle of her back. She put on her new red frock, straightened it and then sat down at the table to wait. There was to be a war between them and she fully intended to win it. But the time passed slowly and he did not come. At length, she decided to go to the river, draw a pail of water and see to her flowers. Never before had she felt like planting flowers – not while she was married to Eogan and it gave her great pleasure to do so now that he was gone.

She was just coming back from the river when she spotted him. This time she would not curtsey and hoped he would take that as a sign of determination. For the past few hours she debated her approach and thought of a range of methods to win her battle from smiling sweetly, to running her sword through him. But just now he looked so handsome seated on his horse, she had to look away to keep from letting her determination dissolve. After all these years, excitement still rushed through her veins at the sight of him.

Macoran watched her carefully pour the water around her flowers and wondered if he dare get down. She did not smile but neither did she glare at him in her normal manner when he came to see her. He decided to take a chance and slowly dismounted, but he kept the reins in his hand instead of tying his horse to a tree branch.

"Good day to ye, Jirvel."

"Why have ye come this time?"

He was relieved. If he knew how to handle any of her moods, it was this one. “Ye did not attend the wedding and I came to see if ye were unwell.”

“Nay, that be not the reason. Kannak would have said if I were unwell. Too much has gone between us for ye to lie to me now.”

“Kannak said ye had a headache. Has it passed?”

“Nay, it was a lie. I wished to avoid Ronan.” She poured the last drop of water and set the bucket down. “Have ye given yer permission yet?

“Nay, but I cannae avoid it much longer. If only ye would tell me whom ye prefer, Jirvel.”

She walked to him and looked him square in the eye. “I told ye whom I preferred years ago.”

Macoran slumped. “That again?”

“Aye, that again. Ye said yerself ye dinna like knowing another man was bedding me. What has changed?”

He stared at her for a long moment and then lowered his eyes, “Nothing has changed.”

“Then ye must not make me marry again. It would be too unkind for us both.”

“But ye must have a husband to care for ye. What will become o’ ye when Stefan marries? And what then when Kannak takes a husband? Ye cannae live alone, Jirvel and ye know it.”

He was right and it took a moment before she could think of a good argument. “What will ye do if yer wife dies and I am again married?”

Macoran closed his eyes in defeat. “I have considered that. Agnes becomes feebler every day, but she be too mean to die. Her hate keeps her alive just to annoy me and I am convinced she will outlive me by many years. I fully intend to haunt that lass once I am dead."

She couldn't help but smile.

Her smiles for him were so rare, he wanted nothing more than to savor the moment. Too soon, her expression grew serious again.

"Please, Artair, ye must find a way not to marry me off. I could not bear it. Ye are the only lad who has touched me and the only one I want to touch me. Can ye not see that?"

She had not called him by his given name in years and it delighted him to hear her say it. He wanted so desperately to take her in his arms, but he held back. If there was to be a touch between them, this time she would have to come to him. "What excuse can I give the lads, Jirvel? Help me think o' a way to do it and I will not betroth ye. But I must have something to tell them."

She put the back of her hand on her forehead, closed her eyes and tried to think of something, but all she could think about was her desire for him. She wanted to run to him, to kiss him passionately and let him take her to that place of exquisite love she had only known once. But another fatherless child would force her to marry again and that was out of the question. "There must be something ye can say, but I cannae think clearly."

"Nor can I." He turned and started to mount his horse. "I will think o' something later."

"Then ye will not give yer permission to any o' the lads?"

"Nay, ye are right. I cannae bear the thought o' another man bedding ye. Be at peace, my love." He put his foot in the stirrup, lifted his leg over, turned his horse and rode away.

She was relieved but she was also miserable and could no longer hold back her tears.

When Blair and Fergus left the wedding feast, Stefan had no more excuses. He mounted Jirvel's horse, gave Kannak his hand and helped her swing up behind him. Half way home, he halted the horse and scooted around a little so he could talk to her. "Why?"

"Why what?"

"Why did no one come to help Eogan with the land? Surely the others wanted to help."

She bit her lower lip and considered a lie. "'Twas not so bad as this till the last year or two. I suppose ye will hear it somehow anyway. My father sometimes hurt her."

"What? And the other lads knew?"

"Some did and no doubt they told the others, but mother begged them not to tell Macoran."

"Why? He be her laird; he should have killed her husband for it."

"Killed him? A laird does not kill a man for hitting his wife."

"I would, especially if he hurt a kind soul like Jirvel. I become enraged at the very thought o' someone harming her."

"Then when ye are laird, I will be pleased to be in yer clan and my mother with me. It was most unpleasant. Ye cannae know the nights I cried for her and…" Tears suddenly flooded her eyes and she could not go on.

He turned a little more and put a brotherly arm around her. "Dinna weep, wee bairn, I dinna mean to upset ye."

She took a deep breath and rested her head on his shoulder for just a moment. Then she drew away, wiped her cheeks and pushed his arm away. "If Macoran knew, he would have shamed father. Then father would have become enraged and we feared he would kill her. There was naught to do but beg the lads not to tell. Father liked his strong drink and dinna know his own strength."

"Did he hurt ye?"

"Once, but mother stepped between us afore he could hurt me much. He was always sorry…later when it was too late."

"Is this why ye have few friends?"

"Mother dinna want people to see her bruises and tell Macoran."

"Then 'tis a good thing yer father be gone. If he comes back, I will kill him myself." He turned back around and urged the horse on.

She put her arm back around Stefan's waist and muttered, "He will not come back."

*

He was proud of their little garden, although it did not grow the volume of vegetables and grain Stefan hoped. He wondered if the soil was different somehow than that in his homeland, but he dared not ask any of the men. Next year, he would spend more time with William and watch how he worked the land. Except for two hot weeks, the rain came often enough to keep them from having to haul very much water from the river to the garden.

The hunting was good, they managed to share the meat of the deer with their neighbors and the women were becoming quite good at making more belts from the skins. All three of them looked forward to the fall festival. After that, they could expect the long hours of darkness and they all agreed a few extra hours of sleep would be very welcome. Perhaps the beautiful night lights in the north would come again in the darkness and they could all lie outside to watch them.

Laird Macoran did as Jirvel bid him, did not betroth her and for the most part stayed away. When he did come, which was only twice during the summer, he kept himself well back, did not ask if she wanted a husband or mention one for Kannak. He only asked if they were in need, assured himself they were not and quickly glanced over the land.

But Stefan had developed a keen eye and an instinct when it came to being watched and every time he felt it, it was Macoran who was doing the watching – from the hilltop, the riverbank or from one of several animal paths. If Jirvel noticed, she did not let on. Instead, she concentrated on making life as easy and happy as possible for them all.

When the first of the vegetables were ready to eat, they celebrated. When Diarmad and Stefan caught ample fish in the river, they celebrated and when Blair brought his baby girl and William and Andrina came to share a noon meal, they celebrated.

For the most part, three happier people in the world did not exist. There was only one concern…Mistress Macoran and her sons were sure to return shortly.

*

Jirvel was not pleased. The priest was asking for a much higher tithe than usual and she was not about to pay it. He sat his horse in her small courtyard wearing a long brown robe made of soft wool with an attached floppy hood over his head and a cloth rope tied around his middle. “Father, was it not ye who said greed was one o’ the seven deadly sins?” she asked.

"Precisely what are ye accusing me o', lass?"

"Not ye father, me."

He got down off his horse, clasped his hands together in a priestly way and rocked up on his tip-toes. "Are ye asking me to hear yer confession?"

"Perhaps, but moreover I am asking ye to help me understand. Is greed not one o' the seven deadly sins?"

"Aye."

"Then I confess I am guilty. Ye see, the good Lord sent us a laddie to help with the land and he needs to be fed. Yet ye are asking me to give over a larger amount o' our food for the tithe and …and my greed forbids it."

The priest studied her eyes for a moment and then gave Stefan a slow look up and down. "Tis a growing laddie at that."

"I dinna know a laddie could eat so much."

As was his habit, the priest started collecting tithes at the eastern edge of Macoran land and worked his way to the village. That meant he would see Ronan next. She handed a small basket of vegetables to him and smiled. "I have heard there are lads who want to marry me, but I think…"

"Ye are already married."

"And happily until recently. But I think the lads who say they prefer me truly want the land instead. 'Tis that not also greed, father?"

He tried to think what she was getting at and hesitated. "But yer married."

"True enough and I wish to stay married. I took a sacred vow and a good wife should wait for her husband no matter how long it takes.

Perhaps he be only lost somewhere."

"'Tis possible, I suppose. A man would be daft not to come back to ye if he were able, Jirvel." He noticed her blush and took the small basket she offered. Then he emptied the contents into a much larger basket tied to the back of his saddle. "Feed that laddie well, Jirvel or ye will answer to me!" With that, he mounted and rode away.

Jirvel smiled. She trusted Macoran not to betroth her, but not letting Ronan talk the priest into setting aside her marriage would be an added measure of protection. For days, all three held their breath waiting for news of Jirvel's marriage circumstances, but nothing more was said and they were relieved.

*

At the fall festival, the belts Jirvel and Kannak made were quickly snatched up. They bartered for a new shovel, two hair brushes the fishermen brought from England and then ordered a new pair of shoes for Kannak and the still growing Stefan. The mood, Stefan noticed was not as lively but then, Mistress Macoran and her wayward sons were back.

As before, Macoran sat on the platform with his wife and watched Jirvel, and just as before she occasionally looked at him. But once they were home and Kannak was asleep, Jirvel slipped out of the cottage and went off some place to cry. Stefan wanted desperately to comfort her, but he wasn't supposed to know about her love for Macoran, so he went to bed instead. That kind of love, he decided, was not worth the pain it caused.

A fortnight later Macoran sent a man. His name was Eachann, and Eachann informed Jirvel that he was to teach Stefan how to fight. But a week later, after Eachann lost every match to Stefan despite the boy's awkwardness, he ventured to speak to Jirvel alone, "The laddie fights like a Viking."

"Many Vikings live in the north."

"I have heard o' a very tall lad in the north, but he be slow o' hand and mind."

"I have heard that too."

"But Stefan be not slow, though I cannae imagine too many lads…even in the north will be as large as he. How old be he?"

"Not yet sixteen."

Eachann shook his head. "He will grow still."

It was the last they saw of Eachann except on their occasional trips to the village.

*

Stefan suffered a growing spurt in the weeks following, his awkwardness increased and the women in his life never missed an occasion to laugh at him. It was time, he decided, to learn the dress of the Scots and once he became accustomed to the belting and tucking, he found the tapered pants comfortable and likeable. Kannak presented him with a new belt and he marveled at how accomplished she had become.

But in the fall, the clan's livestock began to grow thick, warm coats and the heather plant bloomed profusely and cast off thousands more seeds than normal. It was a sure sign of a harsh winter. As well, the water level in the river started to drop. Already the rain in the mountains had turned to snow.

*

It happened on a day when they were bundling fire wood and taking it to the shed. Kannak suddenly let the bundle she carried fall to the ground and grabbed the top of her head. A few yards behind her, Stefan threw his bundle away, ran and got to her just before she collapsed. “Jirvel!”

Stefan already had her in his arms and was carrying her toward the cottage when Jirvel rushed out, felt Kannak’s hot forehead and gasped. “She has the fever.” Jirvel rushed to the door, held it open and then followed him through the first room and into the small bedchamber. She threw back the covers and waited for him to lay Kannak down.

“My head hurts,” Kannak moaned.

Stefan backed away, “What can I do to help?”

Jirvel was already starting to loosen her daughter’s clothing. “Pull off her shoes and then put more wood on the fire. She will chill soon and we must keep her warm.”

He did as she said, closed his eyes each time Kannak complained of the headache and was in a state of near panic. They could not lose Kannak; it would be too cruel for Jirvel. Kannak needed the kind of help he could not give her and although Stefan had not felt Macoran watching them that day, maybe…just maybe.

He stepped outside and started to slowly scan the trees and the paths with his eyes. Then he looked up the hill at Macoran’s favorite place. He could not see the man, but just in case, Stefan raised a hand high in the air. It was not a prearranged signal, but it would have to do. More than a few died from a sudden fever and he was determined Kannak would not be among them. He held his hand in the air for a while longer and then went back inside.

It worked. Shortly thereafter, Macoran burst through the door. "What is it?"

"Kannak has the fever," Stefan answered.

Macoran did not hesitate; he moved the curtain aside and went into Jirvel's bedchamber.

"What are ye doing?" a stunned Jirvel asked.

Macoran felt Kannak's head, pulled her up to a sitting position, wrapped her blankets around her and started to pick her up.

"Ye cannae have her."

"Stand aside lass. She goes with me."

"Nay, ye cannae take her, I will not allow it."

He carefully slipped Kannak through the bedchamber doorway and waited for Stefan to open the door to the outside. "'Twill be a harsh winter and Kannak will spend it in the village where I can see that she lives."

"The whole winter?"

Once he got Kannak out the door, he handed her to Stefan and mounted his horse. Then he opened his arms, waited for Stefan to give him the girl and made sure she was completely wrapped up. "There be an empty cottage now that the elder Andrew has passed. Ye are welcome to come or stay as ye please, Jirvel."

Jirvel stood in the doorway with tears in her eyes. "What right have ye to…"

"I am yer laird and I command it. She belongs to me…" he quickly glanced at Stefan, "just as all the children do. Ye will do as I say, Jirvel." With that, he turned his horse around, nudged the horse's flanks and took Kannak away.

Stefan was pleased though he did not let on. Instead, he opened his arms and let his adopted mother cry on his shoulder. "Macoran did the right thing. Ye said yerself we are out of the medicine for headaches and fevers. It would take too long for me to fetch more and return. Gather yer things and follow them. I will see that the fire be put out, take the cow to William and ask him to come for the chickens when he can. Then I will come."

CHAPTER XI

Stefan was beside himself with worry. Something made him fear if he was not with Kannak and quickly, she might die the way his mother died in his father's absence. She and Jirvel were all he had and he had come to love them both. Once Jirvel was on the horse and headed for the village, he made sure the fire was cold, grabbed his extra clothing, stuffed them in a cloth sack and slung it over his shoulder. Then he took the cow to William and started the long walk to the village. He could have borrowed a horse, he knew, but he did not want to take the time to return it. Once he was there, all he wanted to do was stay with Kannak. Soon he was running more often than walking. Still, it seemed to take forever.

The elder's cabin was much the same as Jirvel's except it had no second room. Nevertheless, the one room was large enough for all three of them to have a bed and by the time he got there, Macoran had already moved two more in. It left little room for the table and chairs, but that was the least of their concerns.

Stefan dropped his sack near the door, knelt down beside Kannak's bed and touched her cheek. It was still very hot. "How does she do?" he whispered.

Jirvel put her hand on his shoulder. "She sleeps finally and I doubt she can hear us." She pointed to the array of bottles and small sacks on the table. “Macoran brings every kind o’ potion and remedy he can find and enters without knocking. But we must take care not to give her too much even if he insists. He may be our laird, but he knows nothing o’ helping the sick.”

“Nor do I.”

“Then ‘tis time ye learn. I must go out. If she moans, hold her hand. It seems to comfort her.” She waited for his nod and then slipped out the door.

Stefan got up, moved a chair next to Kannak’s bed and sat down. She looked so vulnerable and so very ill. He again touched her cheek, but it was just as hot and there was nothing he could do. When she suddenly opened her eyes, she looked disoriented and frightened. Instinctively, he took her hand and when she finally focused on his face and recognized him, she tried to smile. “Sleep, wee bairn, sleep.” She lightly squeezed his hand and closed her eyes.

But he did not let go of her hand. He remembered how affectionate his aunt and uncle were and realized he missed it. They constantly hugged him and even when he got older and protested, they continued to often muss his hair or pat his back. If Kannak were well, perhaps he would not be so bold, but just now all he had to give her was his affection and perhaps somehow it would help.

For three long days, Kannak fought the fever, could not seem to get warm when she chilled and cried out in pain from the raging headache. Jirvel cared for her during the day and then tried to get at least some sleep while Stefan watched over her at night. Macoran came day and night, bringing still more remedies the first day and then beginning to take some away that night. He reported others were ill as well and needed them; the fever seemed to be sweeping through the whole village.

Stefan built the fire hotter when Kannak chilled and then let the embers simply smolder when she was hot. He lifted her head up and forced her to drink as often as he dared, and then held her hand every time she moaned. Just as Jirvel said, it seemed to calm her and it calmed him too. It also let him know when the fever was subsiding and it was not until the third night that her hand felt almost normal.

At last, she opened her eyes and truly smiled at him. "I thirst," she managed to whisper.

He was thrilled, grabbed the goblet by his chair, lifted her head and helped her drink. "Shall I wash yer face?"

"Aye, that would feel good."

Stefan wet a cloth and carefully dabbed her forehead, her cheeks and then her chin the way Jirvel showed him. Again she smiled, which touched his heart in a way he could not quite understand.

Through a small opening in the window covering, the northern lights danced against the wall and Kannak turned her head to watch them.

"Some believe God lives in the north and he sends his lights to assure us he be still there. Would ye like me to take ye outside?" As soon as she nodded, he sat her up, wrapped her blankets around her and lifted her into his arms. To his surprise, Macoran opened the door and he had not even heard the man come in. When he glanced toward Jirvel's bed, she was sitting up watching.

There was not a soul outside except the guards when Stefan carried her into the courtyard. The northern lights were especially beautiful and looked like a multi-colored curtain waving across the sky. He watched the lights and the delight in her eyes for a time, but when she seemed to drift off to sleep again, he took her back.

Holding her in his arms was a time he would remember always and it was another lesson learned - people, even grown men need the touch of another human being. In the days of her illness, holding her hand seemed to help her and at the same time it somehow took away most of the hurt in his heart over losing his father.

*

It was a winter of much sorrow.

Kannak was indeed not the only one to come down with the fever and although she slowly recovered, several of the younger children and even a few of the elders died. The clan's graveyard was located down the beach on the side of the hill. Stefan helped dig the graves and for a time it seemed they completed one burial only to be faced with another.

With the low river water, fishing was not as plentiful and several of the men had to go to sea to find other kinds of fish. Hungry wolves were often spotted too close to the village and fires were lit along the edges to keep them away at night.

Then the snow and ice came.

Even so, Mistress Macoran took her daily walk along the ocean shore still hoping the Vikings would come back. When she wasn't looking for Vikings, she cursed her husband and prayed he would die of the fever. But he did not even manage a sneeze and she was furious.

In her father's village, her sons had been caught twice playing with fire and it was all she could do to keep them in check before they shamed her. For that she blamed Macoran as well. She never should have bedded him and proclaimed barrenness to her father instead. Why did she always manage to think of these things after it was too late? Now she was stuck with a husband whom she hated and two sons she was beginning to care even less for. It was all Macoran's fault and she would make him pay if it was the last thing she ever did.

*

Once the illness left the village, Stefan spent his time gathering wood and dried heather for their fire, went fishing and hunting. He bartered two salmon for a chicken and spent two hours slowly turning the spit to cook it so they could enjoy a special celebration for Kannak's fourteenth birthday. Kannak got better each day but it took three weeks for her to get all her strength back. Stefan took her on short walks at first and then longer ones until she pleaded to be let on her own lest everyone think her a wee bairn still. He reluctantly let her have her way.

For Jirvel, there was another kind of suffering. She stayed inside the cottage most of the time and when she did go out, she avoided going close to the keep or to any place she knew Macoran might be. Seeing him, especially with his wife and children was unbearable. She was pleasant, when she could not avoid her mistress Macoran, but she had no desire to befriend her and prayed the woman did not know why.

*

It was after the snow melted and the weather warmed that Stefan drew his sword and was furious enough to use it. He walked around the corner of a cottage just in time to see Kannak struggling to get free of a man who had his arms tight around her. Stefan's rage was instant. He grabbed the man by the hair and yanked him away from her. Then he moved back and drew his sword. A second later the other man did the same and they both prepared to fight.

Kannak gasped. "Nay, Stefan, he dinna hurt me."

"Go to yer mother, Kannak."

But instead of doing as he said, she saw the other man begin to attack, heard the crash of their swords and screamed. Seconds later Macoran and several other men came running.

"What is it?" Macoran asked. "Why do ye fight?"

Stefan successfully blocked the man's second strike and was about to go on the offense when Macoran arrived. There was fury in his eyes and he did not take them off his opponent even for a moment, "He tried to force Kannak."

"If this be true, I will kill him myself," said Macoran.

"'Tis not true," the other man said. "I only tried to kiss her."

Stefan was not appeased, "Ye dinna kiss a lass unless she be willing."

It was the first time Stefan called her a woman and Kannak set aside her terror in favor of wonder.

"Put away yer swords. 'Twill be no bloodletting this day." Macoran put his hand on the top of Stefan's and tried to force it down. But Stefan resisted and was not willing to put his sword back in the sheath until after the other man did. He held his fierce glare steady, found it hard to let go of his anger and it surprised even him. "Be it not true a lad's family be the only thing worth dying for?"

"Aye, 'tis true, but no one will die this day. This day we anticipate the coming of spring and all that entails, finally." He noticed they had drawn a crowd and turned to the others. "There be nothing more to see." Then Macoran glared at the other man, "I will deal with ye later." Macoran's ire was evident and the man soon hung his head and walked away. "Did he hurt ye, lass?"

She was less interested in her laird than she was in Stefan. "Nay." But as soon as she started to walk to him, Stefan finished putting his sword away, turned and headed down the path toward the river. "Would ye *really* kill a lad if he hurt me?" Stefan ignored her but she was not about to let him get away without an answer even if she had to run to keep up with him.

When the others were gone and Macoran realized Jirvel was the only one near him, he smiled. "That lad loves yer daughter."

She returned his smile. "I know. 'Tis a delight watching him."

"Do ye believe he be the reason she does not choose a husband?"

"I do. 'Tis a delight watching her too." They might have talked longer, but when Jirvel looked, Macoran's wife was watching from the landing. Jirvel curtsied to her laird and walked away.

That afternoon, Agnes was seen walking down the beach talking to herself.

*

The rains followed the snow, but on a clear day when the sun finally began to dry the land and Stefan had gone off with the other men to hunt, there came a fateful knock on the door. Kannak answered it and was surprised to find Laird Macoran standing there. He had not come to see them since her illness.

She curtsied but he gently waved her aside and entered.

"I would speak to yer mother alone."

She looked to her mother for permission, saw her nod, grabbed her warm cloak and left, closing the door behind her. Yet she did not close it completely and was tempted to stay and listen. But when she glanced around, she saw one of Macoran's sons watching from the end of the path. She was not fond of her laird's sons – no one was, and she decided to watch him instead.

How she would have liked kicking both twins in the shins for all the mischief they got into. Once she caught them trying to bore a hole in the bottom of a small boat so it would sink. Another time, she rescued a puppy before they could drown it.

Abruptly, the twin she was watching ran down the path toward her, shot past without even a glance and headed into the courtyard. Too late she suspected the boy intended to tell Mistress Macoran where her husband was and that would surely bring trouble to her mother. All she could do now was watch him dart up the steps and disappeared through the door of the keep. A moment later, mistress Macoran appeared on the landing and glared at Kannak.

*

Inside the cottage, Macoran took a seat opposite Jirvel at the table. "Others have noticed how ye avoid me."

"What did ye expect? Did ye hope I would pretend nothing was wrong? Ye and I are not the only ones who know what happened on our wedding day. Even yer wife suspects there be something between us."

"Agnes dinna suspect."

"She came here."

"What…When?"

"It was on a night when ye stayed away too long. She knocked on the door, entered, looked for ye and then left."

He put his head in his hands. "I have hurt her too. She be as unhappy as we are."

"Impossible…unless she loves ye finally." Jirvel quickly stood up, turned her back to him and walked to the far corner of the room. "My brother wants me to go home and I am considering it."

"Ye cannae. I will not let ye take my Kannak from me."

"When did she become yer's? Save when she was ill, ye have never held her, nor have ye kissed her tears away."

He went to Jirvel and put his hands on her shoulders. "Ye had a husband, remember? Ye cannae know how I longed to hold her and kiss her tears away. If I had, it would only have complicated our lives more."

He was right and when she felt him put his arms around her, she closed her eyes and did not resist. "I have had a great deal o' time to think these past weeks and I realize the fault be not wholly yer's. We were to be married the next day and I saw no harm in it. I went to yer bed willingly and I would do it again, were we given that night back. Kannak be the only good that came from our love and we must do what be best for her."

"And what do ye deem that to be?" He had his eyes closed too and when he opened them, there was more light in the room, than there should have been with the door shut. He let go of her and turned around. There in the doorway stood both his wife and Kannak. His wife folded her arms in a huff, but Kannak turned and started to run.

Jirvel covered her mouth and softly cried out, "Kannak!"

"I will go after her; 'tis time I set at least this much right."

Macoran paid no attention to his wife, walked right past her and headed up the path after his daughter. But when he reached the courtyard, she was already out of sight.

*

The hunt for fresh meat had been fruitless. All the men found were carcasses of red deer the wolves had gotten to and when Stefan came back to the cottage, Jirvel was in a dither, rushing around collecting their things.

"What is it, what has happened?"

She barely glanced at him. "We are taking Kannak home."

"Now? But 'tis not yet spring."

Jirvel stopped packing and closed her eyes. "Ye might as well hear it from me. Kannak be the daughter o' Macoran and she just found out. She has run away, Macoran has gone to find her and I am beside myself with worry."

"I will find her, I know where she goes."

*

Stefan spotted her right where he suspected she would be, at the top of the hill watching the ocean waves. He cleared his throat to let her know he was there but he needn't have bothered. She heard him coming.

"I hate them, I hate them both. They lied to me. I am Macoran's daughter and they did not say."

On the path not far below, Macoran stopped to listen.

"I see, and this be how the daughter o' a laird behaves?"

"The daughter o' a laird, who has never once confessed me. I am bound by no good form to him and I will behave as I see fit."

"Think, Kannak, they did not marry and if he confessed ye, he would bring shame upon yer mother. As angry as ye are, I cannae believe ye would want that."

"Then I am never to know him? All my life I wanted a father who loved me and still I cannae have him?"

Stefan moved to stand beside her, put an arm around her waist and then pointed. "Do ye see that far rock?" He waited for her nod and then continued. "Beyond that, in the waters o' the sea, be where my father be buried. His name was Donar and he was the commander o' a whole fleet o' Viking ships. He died the day ye found me."

She turned to look into his eyes. "Ye never said a word."

"I could not speak o' it till now."

She put her head on his shoulder and welcomed his comfort. "Did he love ye?"

"Very much. The other Vikings came to kill and to steal, but my father only wanted us to run away and build a new life for ourselves here in Scotland."

"What happened?"

"We were running up this very hill when he took an arrow to the back and died. Do ye remember? I took yer horse and left that night."

"Aye."

He gently laid his head against the top of hers, "I came back to bury him but his body was gone. I stood where yer standing now and watched Macoran give him a Viking burial fitting my father's rank. It was a very good and honorable thing for him to do and I have always been grateful. My father be dead but yer's be still alive. For that ye must be grateful as well."

Kannak started to cry, as much to relieve her anger as for Stefan's loss.

"Do not cry, wee bairn. Yer father be a good man and he loves ye, I know he does. Perhaps someday he will manage to tell ye that."

"I want to go home."

Stefan finally realized he was there and glanced Macoran's direction just in time to see him inching away. "So does yer mother. She be gathering our things as we speak. Who knows, maybe the stallion has come back."

Kannak wiped the tears off her cheeks and giggled. "Will we finally give him a name?"

"Ye said so yerself. He be a gift from God and deserves a better name than any we can give him. But we will think on it. Kannak, afore we go back I will have yer pledge."

She lifted her head to look at him and wrinkled her brow. "What sort o' pledge?"

"Yer mother took me in when I had nowhere to go and no family. I will not have ye hurting her with yer words o' anger. What happened could not have been avoided."

"Ye cannae know that."

"True, but there must have been something that kept them apart. Ye have seen the way they are. They love each other still."

She decided he was right and tried to smile. Then she reached up on tip-toe, kissed his cheek and started down the path. "Ye are a good brother, Stefan.

For months, he thought of himself as her brother, but somehow hearing her say it this time bothered him. He was beginning to realize he wanted to be more to her than a brother.

*

Macoran had one more woman to deal with and as soon as he arrived he marched into the keep, went up the stairs to her bedchamber and took a firm hold on both of his wife's shoulders. "Ye dare spy on me?"

"Ye have been unfaithful with that lass for years. Do ye deny it?" She tried to get out of his grasp, but he would not let her.

"I do, but if I were unfaithful, whose fault would it be? Ye dinna welcome me to yer bed."

Agnes laughed a cruel, guttural laugh. "As if ye wanted me to. I had to ply ye with strong drink just to conceive my sons."

"Fortunately for me, I dinna recall that night. But dinna change the subject. I will not tolerate yer spying and yer punishment for doing so is this – ye will not see yer father this year." She gasped and he knew his words hit the mark. "Furthermore, if ye breathe a word o' what ye heard, I will bring shame down upon ye the likes o' which ye have never seen. I will swear ye have committed adultery, set this marriage aside and gladly send ye and yer sons to yer father forever. Do ye hear me, Agnes?" She reluctantly nodded and at length, he let go of her and stormed out of her bedchamber.

Macoran went back down the stairs, poured himself a goblet of wine and sat down at the table. "What mud I have made of everything."

*

Agnes was furious and slammed her door. For years she hoped Macoran would set her aside and at last she had the perfect way to accomplish it. How she would love to shout the news about Kannak from the highest window for all the world to hear and force him to set her aside. But after her mother passed, her father caught his young bride with another man and killed them both. Then he let it be known adultery was not to be tolerated by anyone in his family…not now and not ever.

How very cruel life had been to her, and now Agnes could not even go home for a visit. It was slow in coming but finally, she thought of something…poison. But where was she to get it? She had no one to trust, not among the Macorans. Perhaps if she were pleasant and if she could keep her sons out of trouble, Macoran would change his mind and let her visit her aging father. Aye, there was plenty of poison to be had at the Brodie hold.

CHAPTER XII

Stefan let it slip that he was indeed the missing Viking and wondered what Macoran would do, but Macoran did not come out of the keep before they left, no warriors came to take him away and he assumed he was safe…at least for now.

None of them spoke during their ride home and although he could not be certain exactly when, Stefan realized he must have turned sixteen. The cottage looked no worse for wear, most likely because both William and Stefan had been there to check on the place every time the weather permitted. Stefan used his flint and dry heather to start a fire in the hearth and went to fetch water. Jirvel used her broom to clear away the cobwebs and sweep out the mud they tracked in while Kannak put the food away and then shook their bedding and made their beds.

They remained silent even during their evening meal and then washed their bowls in the bucket of water and put them away. At last they sat back down at the table and there was nothing left to do but talk or go to bed. Kannak opted to do the latter and stood back up, but Jirvel took her hand. "We will say all there be to say and be done with it."

Kannak puffed her cheeks. Her real parentage was all so new, she had not thought it through and the last thing she wanted to do was talk about it. But she saw the look in Stefan's eyes, remembered her pledge and sat back down at the table.

"It was on our wedding day that the Brodie warriors came and surrounded the village. They far outnumbered our men, were ready to fight and we were terrified. If…yer *father* had not done what he did, the men would have been killed and the lasses and wee ones carried off."

"What did he do?" Kannak asked.

"He offered himself instead. Laird Brodie had a daughter no lad was ever likely to marry and yer father knew it. An unattached daughter be an embarrassment to a laird charged with matchmaking. Macoran agreed to marry her in exchange for the lives of his people."

"On yer wedding day? How could he?"

"How could he not?" Jirvel saw the tears welling up in her daughter's eyes and handed her a cloth. "I have sheltered ye, Kannak. Ye do not understand there are evil lads in the world who force a lass for sport. They beat her, shame her and dinna marry her. Yer father saved us from lads like that."

Kannak thought about it for a long time, trying to take it all in. Then she suddenly began to giggle. "Agnes be so unsightly. 'Tis a fitting punishment for him."

Jirvel smiled then too. "The poor dear. And she be married to a lad who will never love her. Her fate be perhaps worse than ours."

"But if she died, would he…"

"Dinna even think such a thing. I have had enough pain and I will not add that guilt to it." She took the cloth back and wiped the last of her daughter's tears away. "All I ask is that ye dinna blame him. Yer father did not do this to hurt ye."

"I will try, for yer sake." She got up, kissed her mother's cheek and headed for bed. But when she got to the doorway, she turned back. "I have seen a sea monster, Stefan."

"When?"

"Just afore ye found me on the hill. It jumped out o' the water and I know it saw me."

"What did it look like?"

"A fish…an enormous fish with a huge mouth. Ye have won the wager and I will take ye to see the hidden castle come warmer weather." She turned back around and went to bed.

Jirvel took hold of Stefan's arm. "'Tis dangerous and we are forbidden to go there. Talk her out o' it, she listens to ye."

*

After the noon meal of the next day when Stefan opened the door intending to fetch a bucket of water from the river, he was shocked to find Macoran seated on a horse in the courtyard holding the reins to a second horse. He had not heard a sound. He worried that he was about to be taken away, but Macoran was alone so he relaxed and stuck his head back in the door. "Laird Macoran be here."

Immediately, Kannak and Jirvel came out and as she always did, Jirvel glared at him. "Why are ye here?"

"I brought Stefan a horse o' his own and I have come to see my daughter." He tossed the reins of the other horse to Stefan and continued, "Come here, Kannak."

She was hesitant but finally walked to him. Then he leaned down, opened his arms and smiled. "Will ye ride with me, daughter?"

She was still uncertain, but she wrapped her arms around his neck and let him lift her onto the horse. She was as stiff as a board with her hands folded in her lap and her legs over one of his when he put his arm around her waist and turned the horse. He did not turn down the path as she expected. Instead, he urged the horse halfway up the side of the hill, found a small clearing, stopped and turned the horse around. Through the trees, she could see the cottage, the land and a little of the river beyond.

"I have watched ye grow up from here."

"I…dinna see ye."

"Nay, ye did not. I was careful not to let ye see me."

She didn't know what to say. Being his daughter was something she had not had much time to consider and it seemed odd to be with him now.

"Ye are trembling, are ye afraid o' me?"

"Nay, not afraid."

"What then? Do ye hate me? Is it impossible to be with me after all the wrong I have done to ye and yer mother?"

"My mother explained it sufficiently."

"Sufficiently. I see."

In the distance, she watched Stefan bring the water back to the cottage and take it inside. Then she turned to look into her father's eyes. "Do ye intend to marry me off?"

"Do ye want me to?"

"Nay, but 'tis what lairds do I have heard."

"Aye, 'tis what lairds do. In yer case, I promised yer mother to let ye fall in love with the lad ye will marry. Have ye fallen in love?"

"I hardly know anyone, save Stefan."

"Do ye love him?"

She was taken aback by his question. "Of course I do. He be like a brother to me."

"Just as I suspected. How shall we let ye fall in love then? Shall I send lads to meet ye or shall ye come to the village often and then do yer choosing?"

"Laird Macoran, I only yesterday became yer daughter and now ye ask me to make too many decisions? I cannae. I am not able to think even."

"I understand. 'Tis just that I have my hands full keeping all the lads away who want ye."

At that she scooted around so she could more fully look at him. "Truly?"

"Truly. Ye have become very pleasing and I venture to say ye may have yer pick. But for my sake, see that he has his wits about him."

She giggled. "There are fewer o' those than ye know."

"I was afraid ye might think that. I had hoped ye might have already considered one or two during yer stay in the village, but I see ye have not. Ye found none o' the lads to yer liking?"

"Oh they are pleasant enough, helpful and considerate, but…"

"But yer heart did not flutter when ye saw them?"

"My heart will flutter?"

"Aye, mine still flutters every time I see yer mother." He sighed, cupped his hand around the back of her head and encouraged her to lean against his chest. "What I would give to have her back. There were days when I wanted nothing more than to come get the two of ye and ride away where no one would know us. But alas, it was an impossible dream. A laird must care for all his clan, not just two. I cannae undo what be done, but …" He paused to find just the right words. "But I can tell ye this; I have loved ye every day o' yer life."

A tear rolled down her cheek. She felt him kiss the top of her head and she could not resist putting her arms around him and letting him hold her more completely. Then she pulled away and dried her tears. "Will ye help me find a lad like ye to marry?"

Nothing could have made him more proud and he took her back in his arms and held her a little while longer. "I will do as best I can."

"But he must be a tall lad with good teeth for my mother's sake. He must be very strong, with..." She was still giving him her list of demands when he got her home and let her slide down off the horse.

Macoran smiled at Jirvel, even though she was still glaring at him, turned his horse and rode away a happy man.

"He promised to find me a good husband," Kannak announced as she walked past her mother and went inside.

"She be but fourteen," Jirvel whispered, as she watched Macoran turn his horse down the path toward the village.

*

It was time to do the marketing. They needed seeds for the spring planting a second new shovel, if they could find one and strong rope. Stefan hoped to surprise them by hanging a swing from the branch of an oak tree. If he could keep them from discovering what he was up to, it would be the perfect surprise.

This time, Jirvel wanted some time alone and promised to come on her horse later so Kannak and Stefan rode the same horse as they so often had in the past. "Up or around?" Stefan asked as they headed down the path.

Seated behind him, she playfully slapped his back, "I cannae believe ye asked me that. Ye know how I like to see the water from the top o' the hill."

"Still? Have ye not yet grown weary o' watching it?"

"I shall never grow weary. After all, I might see another sea monster."

He wasn't sure he believed her on that subject, but he let it pass and turned up the hill. "Why do ye find the water so fascinating?"

"I dinna know. It be constantly moving, first drawing out and then coming back in waves that curl with white foam on the edges. What do ye think makes it do that?"

"Tis the heartbeat o' the great dragon."

Kannak rolled her eyes. "If a dragon were that big, more than just the Vikings would have seen it by now."

"I feel another wager coming on."

"I could wager there are no dragons, but 'tis a wager I could not win and I do so like to win." She tightened her arms around him to keep from falling off the back of the horse as it climbed the hill and remained quiet for a time.

He liked having her arms around him, even if it was just to hold on. He especially liked it when she laid her head against his back and imagined she was hugging him intentionally. Too soon, she was full of questions again.

"What else could make the water move constantly?"

"The wind." He half expected to run into Macoran as he urged the horse upward, but their laird was no where in sight.

"The wind? But 'tis not always windy."

"'Tis always windy somewhere in the world."

Kannak wrinkled her brow. The world she knew only consisted of France, England, Scotland, Ireland and the dreaded land of the Vikings. "How big be the world?"

"The world has no ending."

She clicked her tongue on the top of her mouth. "Ye do not know that, bletherskite? I begin to think ye dinna know everything after all."

"I know there be a place called Deutschland and another they call Istanbul. Deutschland is not so far, but Istanbul is many weeks to the south. The air be far warmer than it be here…hotter even than our summer heat, and it stays hot all the time. The lands in the south have many riches, I am told. They are rich in jewels, gold, silver and…" He saw them just as they reached the top of the hill and quickly halted his horse. Seven Viking ships sat in the water a careful distance from the shore and the men had their oars held straight up waiting for the order to row. He heard Kannak catch her breath and tighten her arms around him.

"They mean to attack again."

"Nay, they will not attack. They have come to find me. Get down, Kannak."

"Nay, Stefan I will not get down."

He turned nearly all the way around, kissed her forehead and then pried her arms away. Swiftly, he lifted her off the horse and stood her on the ground.

"Nay, Stefan, dinna leave us. We need ye still."

"Stay here!"

"Will ye come back?" He did not answer and already tears were streaming down her cheeks as she watched him disappear into the forest.

After nearly a year, they had finally come back for Donar and his son, and they came with seven full ships prepared to fight for them. Yet Stefan did not want a fight. Instead, he traveled in the trees until he was sure Macoran's men could not see him and then rode past the cemetery and down to the sandy beach to show himself. It wasn't long until the ships turned his direction and began to row.

He could hear the men in the village cheering when they turned and hoped the Macoran's would not come to see why, but just in case, he rode further down the beach and then stopped. His heart was overjoyed and he desperately wanted to go home, to carve a stone in his father's memory and to see his aunt, uncle and cousins again.

Six of the ships slowed and stayed off shore while the seventh beached. To Stefan's amazement, Anundi was the first to jump down off the rim of the ship. At the same time, Stefan dismounted and went to greet him. He was pleased to see his old friend…but he had bad news.

*

There was to be a celebration in the village and everyone was excited – everyone but Agnes. She was taking her walk along the shore, was the first to spot the Vikings and never said a word of warning as she calmly went to her bedchamber to hide. But instead of hiding, she hurried to her window to watch. She heard her husband shout commands, wished he had no voice, saw the Limonds line up on the other side of the river and willed their barge to sink. Left alone to fight seven full ships of able-bodied Vikings, surely the clan would lose and more than anything, she wanted to watch her husband die. Then she spotted her sons running as fast as they could…away from the village.

But the cowardly Vikings turned their ships and went away. Once they were gone, she sat down on her bed and wept. Was she never going to be rid of Macoran? What cruelty was this?

Macoran, on the other hand, decided after losing the last battle, the Vikings were too cowardly to attack and his chest swelled with pride. He promised his own store of wine and mead, and then proclaimed there would be laughter and dancing well into the night.

But Kannak was beside herself with grief. She could no longer see the ships, did not know where Stefan was and although he told her to stay there, he did not say to wait for him there or that he was coming back. Yet all she could do was wait. At length, she found the rock he hid behind when she first saw him and sat down. "I refuse to cry another tear. Only wee bairn cry and I…he has to come back, what will we do without him?" Her heart was slowly breaking and the longer he stayed away, the worse it got until she thought she would go daft. Still he did not come back and before dark, she would be forced to walk down the hill to the village and face her mother and Macoran with the truth.

The truth. For a moment she wondered what the truth was. For most of a year, she and her mother had hidden a Viking and although her father…her real father might not condemn them, the others surely would, especially those who had lost men in the Viking battles. Then what? They would be forced to live with her uncle Greagor in the north, she supposed and that meant she would lose her father all over again. Not only that, she would sorely miss Stefan.

The longer he stayed away and the more she thought about the consequences she and her mother would face if he were truly gone, the more upset she became. Kannak finally gritted her teeth, "Ye cannae leave us!"

In the trees just out of sight, Stefan watched her. He had never seen her this enraged before and found it amusing. Yet he knew enough not to laugh and wanted her to calm down a little before he showed himself. Then, just as he decided she was calm enough, she started to cry and he could not bear to see her in tears. He dismounted and led the horse out of the trees making enough noise not to frighten her.

Embarrassed, she quickly wiped her tears away and turned so he could not see. "Mother will wonder where we got to."

"Aye, why do ye cry?"

"I do not cry."

He smiled and offered his hand. "Yer eyes are red, Kannak and ye are not practiced at lying, nor should ye be."

"Ye did not go with them?"

"Alas, I intended to. I miss my family."

"Then why did ye not?"

"Because I realized my father would not be there and 'tis he I miss the most." It was not the real reason but it was not yet time to tell her he loved her and could not leave without her. It occurred to him to take her, but in the end, he could not do that to Jirvel. "Now tell me why ye cried."

She took his hand finally and let him pull her up. "I cried because I missed the horse."

He laughed, kept hold of her hand and started them walking down the path toward the village. "The horse missed ye as well."

"Stefan."

"What?"

"Ye are making me run."

He realized she was right and stopped. "I will try not to do that again."

"'Tis the first time ye promised that. Did ye speak to the Vikings?"

"Aye."

She wanted to hear all about it, but Stefan never talked about the Vikings and did not seem to want to now, so she did not press him. Perhaps someday he would tell her. "I dinna…I…"

"What?"

"Thank ye for not leaving us." She smiled, dropped his hand and hurried on down the path.

Stefan rolled his eyes and patted the horse's nose. "Ye she loves already. Loving me will take a bit longer, it seems."

*

The great hall inside the keep was empty as it usually was when Macoran was away. The twins were elsewhere occupied and Agnes took a seat at the table to wait. But it was not for her husband she waited. Toran hated Macoran as much as she did, having some months' back been caught stealing and publicly whipped in the marketplace where all could see. Not long afterward, she struck up an alliance with him hoping someday she might think of a way out of her marriage and need his help

It was true, she knew about Jirvel, but not until recently did she know the truth about Kannak. Not that she cared how many children her husband had, but Kannak was another pawn in the plot she had been forming in her mind for days. Her only way out, she was convinced, lay in the death of her husband and she thought to poison him, if she could get her hands on the poison. But no matter how pleasant she was and how many times she prevented her sons from getting into mischief, Macoran still refused to let her go to her aging father and without guards, it was not safe crossing Limond land. Therefore, only one answer remained. There had to be a war.

For that, she needed something Macoran would deem worth fighting for and it had to be something so important to him, he would fight in the war personally. Kannak was the answer. The thought of having at last come up with a sound plot made her smile.

Perhaps she might also entangle Jirvel somehow. Macoran would surely leave the village and go off to fight for his Jirvel. Time and time again, she heard her husband refuse to betroth Jirvel to a man who asked for her and Agnes found the whole matter repugnant. His reasons for denying them were unsound and to accept Macoran's answer made his men as witless as he was.

The more she thought about it, the more she believed her plan would work beautifully. Macoran was far fonder of the boy Stefan than he was of his own sons and hopefully, Stefan would die too. Every time Jirvel and her brood came to a festival, Macoran was as happy to see Stefan as he was Kannak and always asked him to join them on the landing. It irked Agnes to the bone.

At last Toran opened the door and came to her. "Ye sent for me, milady?"

"I would have ye take a message to my father and say these words exact. Say…"

CHAPTER XIII

"Yer mother dinna want us to go far away," said Stefan.

"But she did say ye could teach me how to swim. The water in the loch be warmer, there are no currents and we will not stay long." She turned her horse toward the river and did not look back to see if he was following. Kannak knew he would never let her go off alone even if he was convinced she would be safe. When she reached the river bank, she turned west. It would be an easier ride on the path, but then he would see Blair's cottage and know they were off Macoran land.

"I dinna know, Kannak. We dinna tell Jirvel where we were going. What if something happens?"

"Nothing will happen, bletherskite. The lads tend the spring planting and there are none to bother us. Even the hunters have gone farther inland to find food for the village. We will be safe."

Stefan was not so sure. He had a foreboding and could not shake it. Nevertheless, when Kannak had a mind to do something, he was powerless to prevent her – short of physically stopping her, which he had never done even once in the past.

He was becoming less awkward, but he was not in complete control of his strength and feared hurting Kannak more than he feared other dangers. At least the Macorans were not at war with anyone. The trees were thickest near the river and he followed her for quite a distance before they at last came to the loch. The beauty of the pristine water with the mountains behind it thrilled him. This place looked more like the home he left in Scandinavia than any other he had seen in Scotland.

Kannak pointed to the far end of the loch where two steep hills nearly touched the water's edge. "The water be the shallowest at that end."

"Ye have come here afore?"

"With my…Eogan. He brought me and my mother here once when he was feeling kindly. Mother brought bread and meat, spread a cloth and we ate under those trees over there." Kannak turned her horse that direction and led Stefan to the end of the loch. Then she halted and waited for him to help her down.

Stefan tied the reins of his horse to a tree and then went to her. A thousand times in the past he had helped her mount and dismount, but during the last few weeks, he savored touching her more each time. Nearly all of Kannak's freckles had disappeared into the creamy complexion of a young woman. Together with her auburn hair and the deep dimples in her cheeks when she smiled, her complexion served to bring out the brightness of her green eyes and her beauty had certainly not gone unnoticed by him. Each day he more acutely felt her nearness and longed to hold her. If only she would let him.

She too felt a change in the two of them. While she still teased him at every opportunity, she noticed a different look in his eyes and it perplexed her. It was the same look he had now, so when he put his hands on her waist, waited for her to put hers on his wide shoulders and slowly lowered her to the ground, she quickly let go. But he did not let go and she looked up at him. "Why do ye look at me like that?"

"Like what?"

She moved his hands away and slipped around him. "Like ye are seeing me for the first time."

"Ye have change, ye have grown up."

"I thought something was different, ye have not called me wee bairn in weeks."

"Perhaps because yer no longer a wee bairn."

She hid her smile and went to stand at the edge of the water. "Well, I am happy to hear it. I can hardly find a husband if ye keep calling me that."

He tied the reins of her horse and went to stand next to her to take in the beauty of the loch. "Then ye have found a lad ye prefer above all others?"

"Nay, not yet. I begin to believe only a laird will do. I want to be mistress o' all I see and am convinced only that will satisfy me."

"How many lairds are there for ye to choose from?"

She stuck her nose in the air and started to walk around the edge of the loch toward the two hills, "Ye need not remind me o' my limited opportunities. I intend to ask my father to find me one."

"I see. Will ye marry this laird even if ye dinna love him?"

"I can learn to love him."

"Ye will learn to love the power over others he gives ye, ye mean. But what if he be cruel?"

"There are no cruel lairds in Scotland."

He rolled his eyes, "Ye are not so grown up as I thought. There are many cruel lads in the world and some even become lairds."

"Then I will *not* learn to love him." She lifted her skirt a little, stepped over a log and then walked on around the shore.

"If ye dinna love him, ye will make him miserable. What will ye do if he beats ye for his unhappiness?"

She stopped walking to think about that and then turned around to face him. "I will send for ye and ye will come to save me."

Stefan laughed. "Am I expected to kill him for ye?"

"Of course," she said, and was on her way around the loch again.

"I cannae come to save ye."

Again she stopped, turned around and this time she put her hands on her hips. "Any why not?"

"Because I will have a wife by then and I cannae leave her. What would she think o' me going off to save another lass?"

Kannak's demeanor suddenly changed. She had not thought of him taking a wife until now and found it disturbing. She intended to take a husband someday, but she did not consider being separated from Stefan. The thought of them not being together oddly hurt her heart. "What sort o' wife will ye take?"

"I have given that a great deal o' thought. She must be shy when 'tis fitting to be shy, cheerful when 'tis fitting to be cheerful and she must love me. I will not consider a wife who dinna not love me wholly and completely afore I marry her."

"And will ye love her?"

"If I am forced." He passed her by and left her standing there with her mouth agape. Just as he expected, she ran to catch up.

"I curse yer long legs, Stefan Rossetti. Ye are always making me run after ye."

She was right, of course, and it would not do in the future. He wanted to walk with her, talk to her and just look at her when Jirvel was not with them. "I will try to amend my ways, but only for yer sake and none other."

"Thank ye. Now I must know; how can a lad be forced to love his wife?"

"'Tis not easy, I assure ye. But there are times when a lad falls under a lass' spell."

"What spell? Do tell me Stefan so I may use this spell on my husband."

He had already said too much. "Ye are too young still."

"I am a wee bairn again so soon?" She smacked his arm and got ahead of him. "I hate ye sometimes."

He smiled. "I know." It was then he realized what was in front of them. Between the trees he could see some sort of structure. It appeared to be in the crevice between the two hills.

Kannak couldn't help but beam. "'Tis the hidden castle."

"Ye have tricked me."

"Aye, but ye will find it well worth the trickery." She grabbed his hand as she had a million times before, but this time her heart fluttered at his touch, it startled her and she quickly let go. "Come, I will show ye."

"I dinna know, Kannak. 'Tis not safe."

"We need not go in, we will only see it from the outside and then we will leave."

"Alright, but ye will stay behind me just in case." Stefan waited for her nod, pulled his sword and led her through the trees. The closer they got to the castle, the larger it looked until all three stories of the round structure were visible and Stefan stopped. Instead of normal windows, narrow slits, some vertical and some horizontal, were visible in the brown stone and it looked to be sturdy still, unlike some of the older abandoned structures he had seen in his country. The wooden door was the only thing he could see with any damage.

"They say the King o' Scotland once lived here."

"Why did he leave?"

"'Tis haunted."

Stefan smiled. "I am tempted to see this ghost."

"Nay, we must not."

"Frightened, wee bairn?"

"Aye."

Stefan laughed. "Wait here then, but I will see this ghost." He pushed through the last of the tall bushes and walked closer to the castle. He wondered for a moment why he had not seen the structure from afar, but then realized the stones in the structure matched the color of the hills perfectly and the windows were too small to give it away unless a man had a keen enough eye to spot them.

He put his sword away and this time when he took her hand, she did not remove it. It was worth being tricked, he thought, just to have her hand in his. Cautiously, he took hold of the aged leather strap and gently pulled until the door opened a crack. Then he slipped his hand in the crack and opened it wide.

A musty smell greeted them, but it soon dissipated and when he took a step inside and his eyes adjusted to the scant light from the doorway, he discovered the great hall lavishly furnished with a fine oak table and several chairs still intact. A thick layer of dust lay on the table together with wooden bowls containing dry contents that might have once been someone's evening meal.

Caked with dust as well, a once magnificent tapestry still hung on one wall, although a corner of it had come loose. A stone staircase led to the next level and he started toward it but Kannak held back. He squeezed her hand to reassure her. "I see no ghost here; we must go up to find it."

"But what if the stairs …" Suddenly, a low groaning sound filled the whole castle. Kannak gripped his hand, wrapped her other arm around his upper arm and then hid behind him. "'Tis the ghost. Come away, Stefan."

"Listen." He put his hand on her arm to comfort her and waited. He did not have to wait long. When the sound filled the castle again, he smiled. "'Tis a wind chamber."

"A what?"

"A wind chamber. 'Tis like a flute. The roof must have a hole in it and when the wind blows in, it escapes through the narrow windows and makes that sound."

"Well I dinna like it here. Come away, Stefan."

"But I will see the rest o' it." He expected her to let go when he started for the stairs, but she was not about to be left alone and held on. Carefully, he tested each of the stone stairs, taking them one at a time and then testing the next to make sure it would hold his weight. They seemed just as strong as the day they were first laid and soon the two were at the top staring into a room still filled with a bed and the belongings of the last occupants.

"Seems they left in a hurry."

"As should we," Kannak whispered.

But Stefan would not be persuaded and started up the second flight of stairs. When they reached the top and opened the wooden door, the back half of the roof indeed had a hole in it just as he suspected. This room had water damage and there was little left of the previous owner's warped and ruined furniture. Still, there was a hand mirror that was not broken and a sewing basket caked with just as much dust as the furniture below.

He had not noticed water damage on the bottom two floors and wondered why. But then he realized the window slits were level with the floor and if the structure was tilted even a little bit, the water would have escaped through the slits and down the outside wall. "'Twas a clever builder. I should like to be a builder someday. I should like it very much."

"Are ye certain there be no ghost?"

"Aye, are ye frightened still?" She had not let go of his hand and he turned to see the look on her face.

"Not if I believe ye."

"And do ye believe me?"

She looked up at him and narrowed her eyes. "I will only believe ye if ye tell me what sort of spell a lass may cast to make her husband love her."

It was more than he could resist. "I will show ye." He moved too quickly for her to resist, took her in his arms and lightly kissed her lips. Just as quickly, he let go and walked to one of the higher vertical slits in the wall to look out.

Kannak was stunned and for a long moment she just stood there looking at the back of his head. Her heart would not be still and the fluttering did not stop. Was this what her father told her about? Had the man she would marry been beside her all these months? She hoped so. Suddenly she hoped so very much. “Some spell, a lad would have to be a simpleton to fall in love over one little kiss.”

“There be more, but I cannae show ye until…”

“Until what?”

This time he had really gone too far and was not at all certain how to get out of it. “Come look at the view, ‘twill take yer breath away.” She wanted him to take her in his arms again, but when she came closer he moved out of the way.

The light shining through the opening made the side of her hair shine and he watched her smile widen as she looked out across the loch and the land beyond.

“‘Tis beautiful.”

“Indeed it is.” He meant her and when she suspected and looked at him, he looked away. “I cannae teach ye how to swim up here, now can I?”

She sighed and looked out the window once more. “Oh, look.”

He moved to stand behind her and tried to see what she was talking about. “What?” To his surprise, she leaned against him and when she did, he put his arms around her from behind.

“We have changed.” she whispered.

“Aye, we have.”

She covered his arms with hers and closed her eyes. “Is this what love feels like?”

“I hope so, ‘tis a feeling like no other.” He tightened his arms a little and put his cheek against hers.

“Will we be very happy, do ye suppose?”

“I am not a laird, but I will do as best I can to make ye happy.”

“And will ye love me?”

“More than I do now? ‘Tis not possible.”

“How long have ye loved me?”

“All my life.”

She giggled and turned in his arms. “Say the truth o’ it.”

“If ye must know, I was not certain until the Vikings came to get me. I could not leave ye that day…or any other day.”

“I dinna know I loved ye until just now. How can that be?”

He did not answer. Instead he lightly kissed her again. Then she put her arms around his neck and he kissed her the way he had wanted to for months. He felt her cling to him, tightened his arms around her a little bit more and wanted to hold her forever. But something made him glance out the window and his heart stopped. Looking at him from the other side of the loch was the black stallion.

He lightly kissed her again and then grabbed her hand. He did not want to frighten her, but his foreboding was back and it was stronger than ever. “We best go afore ye cast yer spell on me and I cannae leave.”

She didn’t understand what he meant, but she giggled and was happy to be leaving the dust and the spooky castle behind. Soon they were out the door and hurrying through the trees. “Is it the black stallion that makes ye run?”

He realized he was nearly dragging her and slowed down. “Aye, I want to see if he will come to us.”

They were to their horses when Stefan turned around, grabbed her waist and lifted her up. Then he rushed to the tree, untied her reins and handed them to her. "Go home Kannak, there are men in these woods and they are not Macorans."

She gasped and wanted to wait until he was mounted, but Stefan slapped her horse hard and made the mare speed away. Almost as quickly, two men on their mounts broke through the trees and went after her. She glanced back hoping it was Stefan who was behind her, but when she saw the strangers, she kicked the side of the horse hard, leaned forward and increased her speed. "Stefan," she moaned, tears already in her eyes.

He did not have time to mount or even draw his weapon before he was surrounded by ten men, each with his sword drawn. But instead of caring about his own safety, he watched the two men chasing Kannak around the loch. Then to his amazement, he saw the stallion position himself between Kannak and the men. They tried to go around the stallion, but he moved to block them. Finally, the men realized what a fine mount the stallion was, forgot the girl and tried to catch him.

Stefan smiled. While one man relieved Stefan of his weapons, another bound his hands together in the front. It took three of them to put him on his horse and he did not resist. He had a better chance of escape on a horse, even one that was better suited for endurance than speed.

After they began to ride away, he looked back often and when he saw the other two men ride up behind them without Kannak or the stallion, he breathed easier. He then turned his attention to finding a way to escape, but with six men in front, six behind him and a path that was too narrow to get around, the chances were nonexistent. He would have to wait.

He remembered his mother's gold medallion and tried to think of a way to hide it without their notice. It was all he had of her and one of them was sure to take it. Finally, when the path was more narrow still and he was certain no one could see, he brought his hands up to his neck, took hold of the thin strap and put it in his mouth. It was harder than he thought but at length he managed to bite it in half. Then he pulled the medallion out from inside his tunic, worked the strap free and tucked it in the hidden pocket of the belt Kannak made for him. He looked back several more times until he was certain none of the men were paying attention and let the medallion strap fall.

CHAPTER XIV

They rode until the darkness made it too difficult to see, then stopped for the night in a small clearing, built a campfire and untied him just long enough to let him eat. Two of the men went off by themselves and were arguing, but the only words he heard clearly were "Laird Brodie" and "lass." Then he spotted something very odd. One of the men sitting not far from him wore clothing clearly of Macoran colors. He thought he recognized him, but could not remember his name.

Stefan's hands were tied again, although not as tightly as before and he thought he had a good chance of escaping once his captors went to sleep. But wolves howled, kept spooking the horses and few got any sleep at all. When the chances of escape looked bleak, he thought about the feeling of having Kannak in his arms. He slowly relived every second of their brief but precious love and committed it to memory.

*

From the crest of a hill the next afternoon, it was obvious this hold was twice if not three times the size of the Macoran village. Dozens of horses grazed in a meadow behind the village. Beyond that were cattle and farther still, a large herd of sheep; a sure sign of a prosperous clan. Stefan looked for an avenue of escape and decided to run east – If he managed to get away.

They at last walked their horses into the Brodie courtyard and the men pulled him down off of his. The large, square, three story keep cast a long shadow over most of the courtyard, already a crowd was gathering and the old man standing in the doorway of the keep was obviously not pleased. He set his glare on one of the men, who quickly climbed the steps and disappeared inside.

"Ye dare disobey me?" said the old man before he closed the door.

It was not hard to guess who the elder was for his hooked nose reminded Stefan of Agnes Macoran. The rest of his captors and the other clansmen who gathered stared at the door, paid little attention to Stefan and just let him stand there. But some of the women couldn't seem to take their eyes off him. If he'd thought of it, he might have flirted with one or two hoping they would help him escape, but he didn't think of it. Instead, he was trying to guess why his captors were accused of disobeying.

The voices inside the keep got louder and then the door burst open and the warrior marched back out. He pointed at Stefan, ordered him taken away and then demanded the other Macoran be brought inside.

Instead of leaving Stefan tied up somewhere outside, they put him in an empty cottage, unbound his hands and put guards outside his door. The window was small, too small for him to crawl through, there was no furniture and he could do nothing but sit down on the floor. Exhausted after little sleep the night before, Stefan soon lay down and went to asleep.

For four days, Stefan watched what little he could see through the small window. Twice a day he was given a scant meal and he asked questions each time, but all he learned was the name of the clan – they were indeed the dreaded Brodies whom Jirvel said surrounded the

Macorans on what should have been her wedding day.

The Brodies, he decided on the first day, were preparing for war. Their horses were made ready, the men sharpened their swords, and new arrows were quickly crafted. But war did not come. There did, however, come a great shout from the courtyard on the third day. He doubted he would ever learn what that was about.

Day and night he worried. Did Kannak make it home safely, what would they do without him to work the land and did they think him dead? He took to trying to send a mental message to Kannak each night before he went to sleep. "I am alive, Kannak." He had no idea if such a thing was possible, but it was all he could do. He wondered what had become of his horse. The large brown spot on its rump made it distinctive and surely if the Macoran's saw it they would know it was his.

Sometimes he tried to understand why the black stallion seemed to appear just when they needed it most. Was the stallion truly a gift from God as Jirvel said? He found some measure of comfort in the thought that God, by virtue of the black stallion, was watching over the woman he loved and her mother.

On the fifth day, the door opened and instead of bringing him a meal, two men bound his hands again and took him out into the bright sunlight. He was put on an unfamiliar horse, joined with six other bound men and a guard of twenty took them out of the Brodie village. This time, the Macoran he spotted the night of his capture was also bound. He looked hard at the herd of horses as they passed by, but his was not among them and he suspected the mare had already been bartered away.

They did not have to travel but half a day to reach a wide glen and when the Brodie guards handed their charges over to guards from yet another clan, a pouch of money was also exchanged. It did not take long for Stefan to realize he had been sold.

The irony was not lost on Stefan. For generations the Vikings captured many Scots, both men and women, carried them away and sold them as thralls to other nations. So by that right it was only fair Stefan would find himself sold into slavery. Nevertheless, the knowledge did not lessen his panic. Where were they taking him?

Guards pulled him down off the horse and he watched the Brodies take it back across the glen in the direction of their village. Stefan soon found himself walking, which was not easy with his hands bound together. To his great disappointment, the prisoners were marched west, farther away from the ocean and away from the Macorans.

The new captors were harsh men with whips who said little, fed them little, did not unbind their hands to let them eat and bound their feet as well at night. They forced the prisoners to walk up hills and down again, sometimes on paths and sometimes tramping through the woods. The guards stopped to water their prisoners occasionally, but only because their horses needed water and rest.

Stefan kept an eye out for the stallion but it did not come to help him. When they were on the paths, he watched for other men, even men of yet another unfamiliar clan he could cry out to. But he saw no one. It appeared his captors were intentionally keeping them off the well-traveled paths.

Furthermore, the prisoners were not allowed to talk. If they needed relief, they were told to raise their hands. The guards watched them constantly and more than one man was lashed for not walking quickly enough.

The journey took three more days and by the end of it, Stefan's legs displayed a multitude of scratches from walking through the foliage and his feet were blistered and bleeding. In the evening of the third day, they were finally halted and what Stefan found himself looking at fascinated him enough to take his mind off his feet. Over the river, other men had begun to build a stone bridge and the first completed section had a high arch just like the Romans were fond of building. It brightened his mood a little. If he had to be a slave, he could at least learn how the bridge was built.

Stefan expected they were to help build the bridge the next day, and he was right. The guards took the seven to the river where they were joined with some twenty other men. Yet there were almost as many guards as there were captives, they were heavily armed and the avenues of escape looked bleak. The slaves were told to fill the baskets with rocks and carry them to the bridge. It was hard work and now instead of just sore feet, his arms and back ached long before the end of the day when they were at last allowed to eat and rest.

Day after day, he did his work and fretted over what had become of Kannak. If she were unwell, he would not be there to hold her hand this time and if a man tried to force her, he would not … He had to wipe that worry out his mind before he lost it completely.

The portions of food were small and again only given twice a day. On some mornings all they got was a piece of bread. Trying not to think about his hunger was even more difficult than trying not to worry about Kannak.

Night after night he replayed their last moments together, sent his mental message and prayed she was receiving it. When it was dry the slaves slept in the open where the guards could watch them easier, but when it rained they were allowed to sleep under the branches of the trees. Still, he found no avenue of escape. At night the ankle of each man was tied to a heavy shaft of wood with only enough rope to allow him to turn over. As well, the camp fires were kept ablaze, shedding ample light on the captives.

He wanted desperately to talk to the other Macoran, but it was still forbidden, he suspected, for fear they would join forces and rebel. Rebellion, to Stefan's way of thinking was highly unlikely since the strength of the men dwindled with each passing day.

Twice the guards lashed a man for becoming distracted instead of working and it intensified Stefan's desire to escape. If only there were not so many guards. He might manage to take a sword away from one of them, but he could not fight all twenty men and win.

There was some measure of solace when he could observe how the bridge was being built, if only for a moment or two at a time. He found the construction genius and wished he could become friends with the builder, but alas, that was not possible either.

Then he became fascinated with one of the other slaves. The elder was a smaller man than most and daily, Stefan noticed, the man thought of something to smile about. Some days it was the beauty of a flower he managed to pick and tuck inside his belt so he could smell its sweet fragrance later. Some days it was the splendor of a soaring eagle or the speed with which a squirrel scampered up a tree. Once, the old man almost felt the lash for watching ducks swim down the edge of the river.

But most important to Stefan was the man’s smile and after watching him more intently out of the corner of his eye, it was clear the old man often glanced upward and moved his mouth as though he were talking to God. The elder was missing two teeth, was dirty, hungry and exhausted like the rest of them, yet his smile warmed Stefan’s heart and he endeavored daily to work beside the old man just to see it.

They worked even when it rained and at the beginning of Stefan’s sixth week as a slave, the old man slipped in the mud and started to fall. Stefan dropped his basket and reached out just in time to keep the old man’s head from hitting a sharp rock.

Suddenly, Stefan felt the lash of a whip. The pain made him arch his back and in an instant, he spun around. This time when the guard tried to strike him, Stefan grabbed hold of the whip and yanked the guard to him. He stood a good foot taller than his captor, was enraged enough to kill him and the guard had terror in his eyes. But Stefan worked the whip handle out of the man’s hand, broke it over his knee and tossed it away. He looked to see if the old man needed more help, saw his grateful nod and went back to work.

The stunned guard could do nothing but stare at the blood soaking through the back of Stefan’s tunic. He finally recovered his wits, picked up what was left of his whip and considered its usefulness. He decided there was enough of a handle left to strike Stefan a second time and pulled his hand back.

“I would not attempt it, were I ye, Striker.”

The guard turned just in time to see a monk ride his mule out of the trees behind him. He lowered both the whip and his head. “I am

Gowan, father."

"Striker suits ye better. Have ye not heard the words of the Lord? A lad who be willing to lose his life for another will sit at the right hand o' God and pass judgment on such as ye when ye have gone to yer just rewards."

All the slaves stopped working and turned to listen. The riled guard dismissed the monk's words and yelled, "Back to work, all o' ye!"

"Where be yer commander, Striker?" asked the monk.

"'Tis the Sabbath. He be resting."

"Aye, 'tis the Sabbath to be sure. 'Tis the only day I am allowed to ride me mule and see the land, which I consider a good way to rest. Perhaps ye would care to show me where in the Good Book it says these men are not also allowed a day o' rest."

At that, the guard frowned. "I dinna make the decisions."

"Who does?"

"My commander."

"Then ye will go and fetch him for me."

"Fetch him? He will have my head if I…"

"I will have yer head if ye dinna." The monk considered the perplexed look on the guard's face for a moment. "Might I remind ye, ye build this bridge for the monastery. When the Pope hears…"

In a flash, the guard hurried off and the monk smiled after him. Then he turned a scowl on the other guards who quickly turned away and minded the slaves.

The monk was a rotund man dressed in the usual brown robe. His robe was made of wool with a different, although similar shade of brown down the middle, obviously added to accommodate his growing size. He seemed not at all bothered by the rain and even left his attached hood off his head exposing a touch of gray along the sides of his dark, tied back hair. He was comfortable on his mule, would have difficulty mounting it again and so stayed where he was.

It seemed a long time before the guard brought his commander. Meanwhile the rain stopped, the monk got a good look at the men and by the time the perturbed commander arrived, he was furious. "Cleanliness be next to Godliness, have ye not heard? They need to bathe and bathe weekly. And when was the last time they had a fit meal? What do ye give them to eat, a chunk o' bread? God said, 'Man shall not live by bread alone and ye well know it. They are to build a bridge, not die where they stand for lack o' sustenance. When the Pope hears about this…"

At the verbal thrashing, the commander was visibly shaken and could think of nothing to say but, "Stop the work!" He did not even notice that the slaves had already stopped and the other guards were afraid to yell at them.

"That's more like it. Now, let them bathe. Ye've a river for it, do ye not?"

"Aye."

"See they wash their clothing as well. I dare not think what sort o' creatures live in soiled clothing. Cleanliness be next to Godliness and ye well know it!"

"Aye, they will wash their clothing."

The monk was far from finished and narrowed his eyes. "I see, and did ye bring soap for the lads?"

The commander could do nothing but bow his head. "Nay, father, but…"

"And blankets for the lads to wrap up in while their clothing dries."

"Aye and blankets."

"And a fit meal?"

"Aye, but…"

"Ye can plainly see I am not resting this Sabbath, nor will ye, not until ye have seen to the needs o' these lads. Yer striker there has injured one o' them and I required medicine for him. See to it. And another thing, since ye neglected their day o' rest, they will rest tomorrow as well. When the Pope hears about this…"

The commander turned his horse and raced back toward the bridge. When he was out of sight, the monk smiled. "Sit down lads, God did not ordain that tired lads should stand when they can sit just as well." But the slaves hesitated looking to the guards for permission. "They lay a hand on ye and I'll see they are sent to the gallows." That seemed to do the trick and the slaves gladly sat down.

CHAPTER XV

A miracle had come to the bridge and Stefan was relieved to see it.

But the elder man was far more concerned with Stefan's injury than he was with resting and boldly walked to where he sat. He carefully pulled the back of Stefan's tunic out of his belt and looked at the injury. "Tis not so bad," he whispered, even though it was obviously going to leave a horrible scar. The elder was afraid to say more and sorely wanted to thank the lad, but his nod and a prayer would have to do. He found a rock, sat down and closed his eyes.

All the men exchanged glances from time to time and waited. They did not mind. Sitting down was a luxury and they basked in it. But then the commander and two more guards returned with medicine, blankets and soap.

"Where might the food be?" chastised the monk.

"'Tis the Sabbath, the..." At the Monk's fierce glare, the commander again turned and rode away.

At last, the ample monk lifted his leg over, held on to the horn of the saddle and slid down, nearly falling to the ground before he got his balance. More annoyed than embarrassed, he straightened his robe, fiddled with the rope around his middle and tied the reins of his mule to a tree. "Take off yer clothing, lads. Ye've naught to show me I have not seen afore."

He nodded for one of the guards to help him and walked down the line handing out the blankets and the soap. There was not enough soap, he decided, and handed a bar to every other man instead. But each got a blanket and as they began to disrobe, their sore feet together with other sores on their bodies horrified him. "'Tis a sad day when Scots treat lads such as this. The Good Book says an enslaved lad's sores will be tended and they well know it."

Some were new sayings for Stefan, he was pretty sure the good book did not say all that, and he almost smiled as he took off all his clothing and stepped into the water. Water…he did not remember how good it felt and even though it was cold, he welcomed it. He welcomed it until he waded out far enough for the water to touch his wound. Even so, he gathered his courage and his breath, submerged and let the river clean weeks of soil off his body. When he came up for air, the old man was beside him handing him the soap.

If nothing more, Stefan had a friend and he was pleased. He rubbed soap all over his hair and body, and then motioned for the old man to turn around so he could rub the soap on the elder's back. He handed it back, submerged again to rinse off and then started to grab his clothing off the rock to wash them. But the old man already had them and with his eyes, was telling Stefan it was his way of showing his appreciation.

Stefan nodded, got out of the water, wrapped a blanket around his waist and sat back down. Before long, the monk was beside him.

"Lay on the grass on yer stomach, lad, so I may tend yer injury. The Good Book says a lad should not be whipped when he has done nothing wrong and they well know it." But Stefan's back was not the only injury and when the monk saw the condition of his feet and his shoes, he was still more enraged. "A lad cannae walk through the gates of heaven with shoes such as these…and they well know it!"

This time Stefan did smile. Still, none of the slaves dared speak and when the monk clumsily got back on his mule and went away, they were certain the old rules would apply and they would be put back to work, wet clothing and all. But they were left to rest and for the first time in weeks, their evening meal consisted of good sized portions of meat, vegetables and bread. This time when they were told to sleep, they all slept like babies and the next morning, the guards were there but no one woke them. It was beyond belief – they were to get a full day of rest. Their miracle was not freedom, but it was the next best thing and Stefan was convinced it was because the old man asked God for help.

In the days to come, the monk returned, checked their injuries and measured all the men for warm winter clothing and new shoes which were delivered just a few days later. Each Sabbath they were allowed baths and a day of rest. More importantly, each meal was hearty enough to improve their health considerably.

As he grew stronger and the routine seemed to hold, Stefan made his plan. The next time they were to bathe in the river, he would simply submerge; swim as long as he could under water and get away. He would have to find a way to cover his nakedness once he was out of the river, he knew, but it was the least of his concerns. As though they read his mind, the guards took to tying two men together at the ankle when they bathed and he was always paired with the old man. As well, they loaded their longbows each time and the fear of being shot in the back like his father weighed heavy on Stefan's mind.

With improved health, even the work got done faster and seemed a bit easier. Still, the work was exhausting, men were lashed when they got distracted, bows were drawn by the guards when they bathed and no possibility of escape presented itself.

The second arch in the bridge was completed by the end of summer.

When fall arrived they were given skins with which to make crude individual shelters under the limbs of the trees. It wasn't much, but it was more than they had before and it offered some measure of privacy if a man finally succumbed to his tears. Stefan did not but he was tempted to.

In his more desperate moments, he wondered if God had forgotten him or if he had committed some unspeakable offense, but Stefan could think of no sin that serious. At length, he remembered to be grateful God was protecting Kannak and Jirvel instead. It seemed to ease his mind considerably.

The privacy of the skins made it easier for a man to untie his hands and feet and then make good his escape. Three tried and met their deaths before they got to the edge of the encampment. There were simply too many guards and as badly as Stefan wanted to, he was not willing to die in the attempt. He wanted to get back to Kannak and live long enough to make her his bride.

The third arch was finished in late fall and winter lay ahead. He was not allowed to ask what day or even what month it was and the marking of time was only certain in the seasons and the passing of each Sabbath.

The good thing about winter in Scotland was the lack of daylight which meant shorter hours of work. That gave the slaves more time to develop a language without speech using their hands and their eyes. The slow closing and opening of the eyes meant a guard was coming and the faster blink meant the guards were going away. Still, he knew none of their names and nothing about them.

They were together, but each man was alone in his thoughts and the loneliness was sometimes unbearable. They could roll their eyes and make very slight hand gestures, but unless they were willing to face the whip, they dared not do more.

The bad thing about winter was the slowness in which the fourth arch was completed and the number of hours Stefan had to fret over Kannak and her mother. Winter meant he had been away for nearly a year and surely they thought him dead. He still sent his nightly mental message to his love, but he had a nagging fear she had chosen another and married. The thought of another man touching her made him furious and now he understood how Macoran felt when Jirvel married Eogan. It was a torture worse than being enslaved or even whipped.

On one Sabbath, the other Macoran slave took sick and was dying. Because the guards were afraid to tend him themselves, Stefan was allowed. He longed to know the man's name if for no other reason than to report his death to the Macorans someday. He soon learned the man's name was Toran and there was not a guard among them who could stop a man from talking in his feverish madness. Toran had plenty to say and before he passed, Stefan knew exactly what had happened and who was behind his capture. He was enraged.

Then the daylight began to lengthen again, the chill in the air lessened and sometime during the building of the fifth and final arch over the river, Stefan turned seventeen.

They were now only twenty-three slaves, for more died including the old man who succumbed to his age and passed peacefully in his sleep. For as long as Stefan lived, he would not forget the smile on the old man's face at the moment of his death and after careful consideration, guessed the angels had come to get him. For a long time after, he wished he had braved the guards and asked the elder's name. He missed the old man's smile, his only comfort on some days but at least his friend was finally relieved of his labors.

It also occurred to him that the old man had the answer to loneliness. There *was* someone he could talk to in his oppressive world of silence. At first he felt too shy to talk to God and said all the things he was taught to say by the priests. But he soon found those words had little meaning when what he really wanted to do was talk to him man-to-God. He asked a thousand questions, requested a million blessings and even thought to barter his freedom, though he had little to barter with save promises.

Some days his mind was too muddled to have a civilized thought, and some days he was too enraged. But in the end, he was certain God had sent the monk to them with warm clothing, food and a bath when they needed it most. Perhaps all he had to do was wait for God's deliverance. But what could be taking so long?

After the elder died, Stefan was paired with a stronger man when they bathed, but this man was not about to submerge under the water. Stefan was certain the man did not know how to swim and in fact, feared the water.

Then spring became summer.

At night he remembered to send his mental message to Kannak and sometimes she would come to him in a dream. The dreams were always different. Sometimes she was in a meadow, sometimes she was laughing at him and sometimes she stood at the top of the hill watching the ocean. But always the dream ended with her hand outstretched to him. It comforted him while at the same time tortured his heart. If only he could get word to her somehow. The fear of her marrying another increased, so he took to sending a message to her every morning as well, "Wait for me, Kannak."

*

When blinks were not enough, the slaves developed a system of whistles and the loudest was to warn of danger. Stefan had noticed the two slightly leaning trees by the river before and after a full week of rain, the ground was loose enough to let them fall. Then when the wind began to blow hard and the trees began to sway, he whistled as loud as he dared. The sound alerted the slaves, but the guards had not yet caught on to the whistles and one threatened to lash him. He lowered his eyes submissively, went back to work and prayed the guard would let his infraction pass. He did. Then Stefan looked at the man next to him, glanced up at the trees and soon the silent word to stay away from them was passed from slave to slave.

One by one, the slaves moved to safer locations and still the guards did not notice how much danger they were in. Two stood directly beneath the trees talking and paying no attention. Then Stefan heard the fateful crack, cupped his hands and yelled, "Run!"

Two other slaves pointed at the trees and just in time, the guards realized what was happening. They scrambled out of the way right before the largest of the two trees fell and kept running until they were well away. Then they looked back in time to see the second tree crash to the ground.

Out of breath, the two guards were stunned. "We surely would have been killed," one of the guards said. He stared at Stefan for a long moment before he finally nodded his appreciation.

That began a measure of respect between the guards and the slaves. It also helped the guards look good in the eyes of their commander. Not many days after, the guards looked the other way and let them exchange names. The man Stefan bathed with was named Baodan.

When food was more scarce than usual, Stefan shared his with those who looked like they needed it more and the men were always grateful. This too the guards allowed, looking the other way when Stefan got up to scrape a portion of his into another man's bowl.

*

It was on a sunny day that two of the slaves delivered their basket of rocks to the top of the bridge, fell off and plunged to their deaths in the water below. It was not an accident, Stefan knew, for one man suffered such great despair daily, he suspected he would try to kill himself. In his attempt to save the first, the second man fell with him. At least this time Stefan knew their names and should he ever escape and find their families, he intended to notify them.

Summer turned to fall and the bridge was finally nearing completion. They had to be set free, they just had to be and Stefan was exceedingly hopeful.

*

Laird Limond was a stout man with a wide girth and sandy hair. His eyes were blue, his mustache was neatly trimmed and he prided himself on always wearing clean clothing. He was also a wealthy man who ruled over a clan of nearly three hundred. He owned the land south of the river that divided him from Macoran and of the Macoran, he was not fond.

Limond's wealth came from the English unquenchable desire for lobster and salmon. The lobster was easy enough for his fishing boats to gather just off the coast of Scotland, but the salmon was another matter. He suspected the Macoran gathered far more than their share when the salmon swam up river to spawn and if he could, he would make a mark down the middle of the river to keep them off his side.

Alas, it was impossible to prove and Macoran always swore they were not guilty, but Limond didn't believe a word of it. Macorans sold their salmon down the coast of England at the very same fish market his men patronized and they always had plenty to sell. It irked him six ways from Sunday.

He once tried to make an alliance with Macoran and the man was willing, but then Macorans were caught red handed with salmon he was certain was from his side of the river and all negotiations were off. A marriage between them was out of the question too once Macoran married the Brodie woman. Besides, Limond had no daughters to give.

Even without the catch the Macorans stole, he was extremely wealthy; his clan had all they needed and most of what they wanted. Therefore, Limond decided to build himself a castle – not just any castle, but one that was high enough to see the river and watch the Macorans. However, the wealth of his clan tended to make his men slothful if not downright lazy and to build a castle, he needed strong men.

When word reached him of a crew of twenty or so felonious men used to build a bridge in the west, he was thrilled. These convicts, he believed, were not truly wicked for what laird would let the wicked live? These were simply thieves and beggars paying for their crimes. So he sent the price and secured the men together with a number of guards. It was a king's ransom he paid for the guard services, but he could afford it. Nevertheless, the bridge builder had other commitments and Limond had to put out the word in search of another.

While he waited, it took twice as long as it should have for his men to clear the land. He was not pleased. At least there were plenty of rocks nearby and if need be, he could send the men to the river to gather them. That, of course, was not his pleasure for surly Laird Macoran would hear of it and it was none of that man's business.

*

This time when they were moved to the new location, the slaves were put on horses compliments of their new master. Stefan was devastated they were not immediately set free, but after they were mounted his mood began to change. They were going east and east took him closer to Macoran land. His hopes were high and as he always did, he tried to find a way to escape. On a horse the prospects increased but the guards were not stupid men. A long rope from horse to horse made it impossible to race away unless there was ample room and all the slaves bolted at once. The paths were too narrow, there was no signal between them should they come to a wide clearing and he doubted it would work anyway.

He watched for Macorans, for the black stallion and for any sign of a village but again he saw nothing. Nevertheless, he did manage to examine the hair of his horse and discovered no thick undergrowth that would signal a harsh winter ahead.

*

It took five days to reach their new destination and their path took them across three rivers. When they at last arrived, Laird Limond was there to meet them. "Ye will first build a store house over there." He pointed to a cleared parcel of land. "'Tis where ye will sleep till the work be done." He looked over each man, decided they were fit and rode away.

He did not identify himself and Stefan was not at all certain where he was. He thought he could smell the sea air, but feared he was imagining things. He could be anywhere either north or south of the Macorans and not know which.

A shelter to sleep in was too good to be true and there was not a man among them who was not eager to begin the work. The new builder arrived and in a few days they had the walls up and the thatched roof ready and hoisted on top. But something was wrong and Stefan knew it.

Their first night sleeping inside was astonishing. The guards bade them to lie down and did not bind their hands and feet as usual. Instead, the guards simply went out and closed the door behind them. At first, the slaves could not believe it and feared if they spoke, the guards would burst back in and lash them. But as the moments passed, one of them whispered, "A curse on them."

They held their breaths to see what would happen, but no guard burst in and they were not caught. Still, they were afraid, exchanged glances for a time and then Stefan became emboldened. He kept his voice very soft, “The new builder knows not what he be doing.”

“Aye,” Baodan whispered. “We are in more danger here.”

No one else said anything and soon they were all asleep. The next morning, they began work on the castle. That night, they were again able to whisper to each other and this new freedom overwhelmed and delighted them.

CHAPTER XVI

In this new place, the slaves occasionally saw women, which was something none of them had seen for more than a year. At night they wanted to discuss them, but Stefan would not let them. “Save yer whispers for important things.”

“Like escaping?” Baodan asked.

“Aye.”

“We could give a false whistle and make them run. Then we could run the other way.”

“And then what?” asked Stefan. “They have horses and we do not. ‘Twould not take long for them to hunt us down and we have no weapons.”

“We could all run in different directions. They cannae hunt us all.” Manachan turned on his side and pulled his blanket up over his shoulder.

Stefan stared at the ceiling thoughtfully. “Aye, but we would have a better chance on horses. We need to know where they keep them.” He heard each man whisper his words to the next, and when he could hear them no more, he went to sleep.

*

Knowing nothing about keeping slaves, Limond let the guards set the rules. The captives were put to work hauling rocks, mixing sod and laying the stones. Just like Jirvel’s chicken pen, the walls consisted of two parallel rows of stones with the sod poured in the middle and allowed to seep between the rocks. Until the sod set, some of the slaves were charged with wiping the excess away from the outside of the rocks and tossing it back in. But the sod was slow to set and the work was hard.

Calluses on their hands and knees bore witness to their labors and the only saving factor was the approach of shorter days. Still fearing the Pope would find out, the guards gave them adequate food and a day of rest in which they were taken on a foot bridge across a river to the edge of a loch to bathe.

*

Laird Limond was not an unsightly man although he was getting on in years. His hair was graying at the sides and Stefan guessed him to be well into his fifties. Being the biggest of all the slaves, it didn't take long for Limond to spot Stefan and when he looked at him, he was impressed with the lad's lack of cowering. Then he spotted Stefan's unique leather belt and motioned for him to turn around so he could see the back. He did not say anything and was soon on his way.

Stefan remembered to breathe. He often touched the belt Kannak made for him. It made him feel closer to her somehow and he would not give it up without a fight.

*

It was during his fourth bath in the loch that he looked toward the very end and noticed two hills near the water's edge. He had to be imagining things. Just above the trees he thought he could see the very top of the hidden castle. He quickly looked away in case one of the guards noticed.

Again bound to the man afraid of drowning, Stefan longed to go closer but Baodan would not budge. It was just as well, the guards were watching them too closely anyway. Nevertheless, he scanned the land again hoping to at least see the black stallion. But the horse was no where in sight. At least now he knew where he was and Kannak was not so very far from him. His desperation to escape increased.

Their nightly talks always centered on a possible way out and the slaves decided they could cut a hole in the roof, stand on each other's shoulders and go. If they were quiet enough, they could get a good head start. But then what? Scatter, they agreed. Surely if they ran in different directions the guards would have more trouble catching them…at least all of them. Still, they needed to know where the horses were and none of them had an answer, nor did they have anything to cut the hole with.

Stefan never said a word about the castle. If he managed to escape, that was exactly where he intended to go and he didn't need a horse. He would swim the loch to get there and this time, he would not be bound to Baodan. Even if the guards spotted him, who would dare enter a haunted castle? He tried to remember if he saw any weapons on the walls and believed he had.

When the wind blew, he sometimes paused to see if he could hear that groaning sound coming from the castle. He could not.

*

As the weeks wore on, Limond's castle grew taller with one level completed and then another. Still interested in building, Stefan considered the construction a complete disaster, and was learning what not to do. If he could not be a builder, he could at least dream of someday being one. It made his days easier somehow.

But his nights were still torture. He longed to hold Kannak just once more. Even when his feet were sore and his muscles ached, he could not get Jirvel and Kannak out of his mind. How had they managed without him? He did not think Jirvel would take a husband even if she were free and he did not like the idea of the two of them being around any man Macoran chose to help them with the land. But what choice did Macoran have?

Then he began to worry Kannak had forgotten him after all this time. She must think him dead by now and how could she not choose a husband? Even worse, how long would Macoran keep his word and not force her to marry? One moment Stefan charged himself to forget her and the next he felt so defeated he wanted to make a run for it, let an arrow in the back claim him and put an end to his misery.

Too soon, it was morning again and there was work to do.

On the next Sabbath while they bathed, Stefan saw two eyes staring at him from behind a bush. He walked out of the water and tried to get a closer look, but Baodan wanted to dry off instead. Just when he was about to give up, a gray wolf ran from behind the bush, stopped, looked at him and took off again. For Kannak ye send a horse, for me it be a wolf, he thought. If only the wolf and the horse could speak.

The next day, they were taken to the river to gather rocks. It would have been easy to swim the river to the Macoran side, but the guards positioned themselves between the slaves and the water. Nevertheless, when he could, Stefan looked for Macorans on the other side. If they were there, they were well hidden. Even if they did see him, he was certain his straggly beard and hair would prevent anyone from recognizing him. He decided if he spotted one, he would chance the lash and cry out, but too soon, they were taken away. Someone had found another rock quarry.

At last the days began to lengthen, the winter had not been harsh and sometime between winter and spring, Stefan turned eighteen.

Surely by now Kannak was married and he should forget her – but he could not. He remembered her challenges, her dimples, the way she looked perturbed when he called her a wee bairn and the feel of her lips when he finally kissed her. He remembered every second of the days they had together and even longed to hear her call him a bletherskite. He was so close to her and still he could not reach her or get word to her. At last, he'd had enough of slavery and cared not if he lived or died. What was life without Kannak anyway?

*

Laird Limond came daily now that the work was progressing faster. He was pleased with his new home and eager to live in it. Yet each time he came, he sought out the location of the tall lad with the pleasing belt.

Stefan glared at him and when Laird Limond came closer, he finally spoke his mind. "Yer castle will fall."

Limond returned his glare, "Dare ye speak to me?"

"'Twill not last a year afore it falls."

Again Limond narrowed his eyes. "Do ye put a curse on it, Lad?"

"Nay, I speak the truth. It will crumble to the ground."

"Ye *do* curse it. I should have ye flogged for saying such as that." His anger remained in his eyes for a time and then his expression mellowed, "But I am not a cruel lad. I will have yer belt instead."

"Nay, ye will not." Two of the guards drew their swords and he could tell by the look in their eyes they meant to use them. Perhaps he did not want to die after all. At length Stefan relented and began to untie his belt. As soon as it was free, he handed it over, grabbed the top of his pants, and held it around his waist to cover his nakedness. His rage was increasing and this time he was bound to lose control.

Limond ignored Stefan and admired the craftsmanship on the outside of the belt, but when he flipped it over to look at the inside, the medallion fell to the ground.

Stefan caught his breath. "'Tis all I have o' my mother."

Limond stooped over, picked up the medallion and was about to toss it away when he thought he recognized it. He stared at it for a while longer and then looked at Stefan's face as though for the first time. "Who be yer mother, lad?"

"She died when I was a wee laddie. Her name was Sheena."

As if he'd been struck, Limond took a step back. For a seemingly endless moment, he again studied Stefan's features. At last, he handed the belt back and turned to the guards. "Let him dress and bring that lad to the keep."

The guards were almost as surprised as Stefan but they did as he said. Stefan was happy to have the belt back, but Laird Limond kept the medallion and he wanted it back too. His rage was quickly returning.

*

Laird Limond's keep was dark and unfriendly. The stuffed head of a wild boar hung on the wall as did several dangerous looking weapons, one of which was the biggest sword Stefan had ever seen. The furnishings were crude and worn through with animal skins spread out on the floor. No wonder the man wanted a castle, his conditions were dreadful, Stefan thought. But he was not there to approve or disapprove of how the man lived, he was there to get his medallion back and he was ready to stand his ground.

He was not bound, but four guards with their swords drawn stood behind him blocking the only door to the outside he could see. All he could do was wait and it seemed like forever before Limond entered the room from behind a curtain.

Limond laid the medallion down on a table and poured himself a goblet of wine. Then he picked the medallion back up and took a seat at the table. "I will hear what ye have to say." He paused to think of just the right question. "Do ye have any other family?"

"I have only one aunt and four cousins, but they do not live here."

It was the right answer and Limond held his breath. "And yer aunt's name?"

"Murdina, she be my mother's sister."

"And she lives still?"

"The last I heard o' her."

"When was that?"

"Two years." Stefan could not understand why the man wanted to know, but at least he was being allowed to talk. "What will ye do with the slaves once yer castle be built?"

"Sell them."

It was just as he expected and it irked him. "They have families."

Limond had not actually thought about that and he dismissed it now. "Tell me, why do ye say my castle will fall? Have the slaves impaired it?"

"'Tis not the slaves who decide the parts to the sod. Yer builder mixed it too thin and it will not hold. If ye let us speak, we would have told ye long ago. Now 'tis too late."

"If I let ye speak, ye would rebel?"

Stefan narrowed his eyes, "If there were a way to rebel, we would not need to speak to plan it. We have no weapons, no horses and we are men who wish to live another day hoping to see our families again."

Limond let Stefan's words hang in the air. "Do ye have a wife and children?"

"Nay, but I would have by now, had I not been snatched."

"Who snatched ye?"

"What does it matter?" Stefan did not mean to let his anger show so forcefully and he feared he would never get his medallion back if he did not calm down.

"Why were ye taken?"

"Macoran's wife arranged it."

"Macoran? What does Macoran have to do with it?"

"I lived with them for a year. I will have my medallion back."

Limond got up, walked to a window and stared out. He had a dozen questions and did not know what to ask first.

"I will have my medallion back," Stefan repeated.

"And ye will get it, but I have something to show ye first." Limond walked to him and put the medallion in Stefan's hand. Then he reached into the pouch he had hanging around his neck and produced another just like it.

Several times, Stefan looked at his and then compared it with the one Limond held. "They are the same."

"Aye. I had one made for myself, my wife and my two daughters,

Sheena and Murdina."

It was Stefan's turn to stare. He wrinkled his brow and tried to accept the words. His mother might have looked like Limond, but he did not remember her face. Still, he remembered his aunt's face and the resemblance was there. "I am yer grandson?"

"It would appear so."

Stefan should have been delighted to have found his grandfather, but he wasn't. Instead he became even more enraged. "Ye have enslaved yer own grandson."

His words bit into the old man's very soul and the color drained out his face. "I dinna know."

"All the slaves are someone's grandson."

"But they are rogues. Slavery be their punishment."

"If it pleases ye to believe it."

"They are not rogues?"

"We are not allowed to speak, remember? If they are rogues, they have more than paid the price for their crimes. Produce the accusers who say differently."

Limond hung his head. "I cannae."

"Then ye must set them free. Yer castle be hopeless and ye have no more use for them."

"But I have paid…"

"Ye have paid?" Stefan's voice was getting louder and he didn't care. "How many nights have ye gone to bed in so much pain ye could not sleep? How many nights have ye laid awake wondering if the lass ye love had chosen another? These lads think of nothing else. They have paid a far higher price for yer castle than ye ever could. Free them and do it today."

"Ye dare command me?"

"Someone must. Ye may be my flesh and blood but ye have become a hardened man with no soul. Murdina remembers ye as a dear father who filled their lives with love and laughter. She said…"

"And was it not yer father who took them…and all the love and laughter with them?"

He was right. Stefan closed his eyes and could not think of anything else to say.

"Yer grandmother passed the very night they were taken. 'Tis what killed all my laughter."

Stefan said it so softly he barely heard the words himself. "Being slave to ye has killed mine."

They seemed to be at an impasse and neither of them knew what to do about it. Finally, Limond got a good look at Stefan's worn clothing and untrimmed hair. "Ye will bathe upstairs in a warm bath and ye shall wear the colors o' yer true clan."

"I will not be yer grandson until ye agree to free the slaves. If ye sell them, ye will sell me as well."

CHAPTER XVII

Not an hour later, Stefan was bathed, his beard and hair were trimmed and he wore new clothing in the colors of his grandfather. The slaves hardly recognized him as he sat a horse next to Limond and looked down at them. "Ye are free. Laird Limond has agreed to give each of ye a portion of food and a horse to see ye home safely."

Limond nodded to the guards, who were happy to walk away, but the slaves still could not believe it. "We are truly free?" asked Baodan.

Stefan smiled. "Aye, and if ye still have families, they have waited long enough."

"And if we no longer have families, where will ye be?" Baodan asked. "I will be in yer clan, Stefan. Ye have saved our lives more than once and ye will be my laird."

Amazed, Stefan watched several of the others nod their agreement. Marriage to a laird was what Kannak wanted and it was now in his power to give it to her. "First I must marry the lass I love…if she be yet free and then I will take her to the hidden castle. Do ye know where that be?"

Limond smiled. "'Tis on my land and ye are welcome to it. The place be haunted."

Several of the men gasped, but Stefan grinned. "'Tis not haunted. 'Tis only the wind, but there are no cottages for ye to live in."

"We can build cottages easy enough." Baodan dumped his last

load of rocks out of the bag he carried over his shoulder and grinned. "Say it again, are we truly free?"

"Truly," said Limond. "My grandson has shown me the error o' my ways and I hope someday ye will forgive me."

"We can go, right enough," another man said, "but we have no weapons to defend ourselves. I'd not like letting them capture me a second time."

At that Limond scratched his head. "I have a few Viking weapons if that will do. Come to the keep and choose. If ye will stay the night, it will give our lasses more time to bake bread for yer journey."

"Do ye trust him, Stefan? Be it a lie?"

"I trust him, but I promised we would not harm his people. 'Tis a small price to pay for our freedom, do ye agree?" He waited and one by one, the men nodded. "Good. If ye come to me at the hidden castle, I will welcome ye and yer families. But let it be known we have nothing to build with, no planted fields and no seed or stores for the winter."

Manachan grinned. "My father will give us seed for planting, he be a right dead brilliant farmer."

It was the first of many smiles Stefan would see that night and he stayed with the slaves even though he wanted nothing more than to swim the river and go to Kannak. He talked to each man, learned of his family and found his nature pleasing. He asked each why they were sold and most of their stories were more like his than of any crimes they committed. Only two admitted stealing. Each claimed it was the Brodies who sold him.

"Our new home will border Brodie land," Stefan warned.

"Good," said Manachan, "I've a message to give them." All the men laughed and their laughter sounded like music. It was nearing dawn when they finally settled down enough to sleep.

The next morning, Stefan watched each choose his weapon, mount his new horse and accept his bag of food. Then he watched them ride away together and at last, it was his turn.

*

The shortest route between his grandfather's side of the river to the Macoran side was to swim, and in summer the water did more meandering than rushing. He rode his grandfather's horse down the river bank until he was sure he recognized the other side, dismounted, handed the reins to his grandfather and then waded into the water. It was ice cold but he didn't care. All he could think of was getting home.

The currents were stronger than he expected, but nothing could defeat him now and he swam hard to reach the other side. He climbed out onto the flat rock where he often filled the bucket with water, paused just a moment to catch his breath and then stood up. His first hint that something was wrong awaited him there. Jirvel's bucket was half buried in the sand along the shore. He stared at it for a moment, pulled it free, dumped out the sand and then rinsed it in the river. That's when he noticed a hole in the bottom, tossed it away and smiled his relief. "Cast off, were ye?"

He almost forgot, turned to wave to his grandfather and then headed up the path to the cottage. But his foreboding was back and the closer he got, the more certain he was that something was wrong. The land looked deserted and the heather had nearly overrun the place again. He finally dismissed that too; perhaps Jirvel would not let Macoran give her a man to help them.

He should have been able to see the cottage by now and when he could not, he slowed. Careful to walk quietly, he eased closer until suddenly he stopped dead in his tracks.

Jirvel's cottage had burned to the ground.

Stunned, he stayed where he was and stared at the ruins. In all his months of worry, he never once considered that the cottage had burned or that his women were in it when it did. He ran his fingers through his wet hair and tried to push the terror out of his mind. Please God, do not let her be dead. At length, he moved closer. But he could not make himself look inside ... not just yet.

Even the shed was burned. Slowly, he walked around what was left of the cottage to the remains of the shed. Even the three walls of the chicken pen were scorched. Burned stubs still remained of the posts that held up the front of the roof and when he dug down, the pouch with his father's gold and silver coins was still there.

Stefan stood up and shook the dirt off the pouch. Then he checked the contents, hung it around his neck and slipped it inside his tunic.

Finally, he forced himself to look at what remained of the cottage. There was little left but the outline of the walls and the hearth. He went back, paused at the doorway and then stepped inside. Jirvel's little basket of salt still hung on a hook on the hearth, but the outside of it was black. He could see the charred remains of everything that had been made of metal and carefully stepped over them toward the small room the women used as a bedchamber.

He did not want to look, but he had to know if there were any recognizable human remains. When he saw none, he was comforted. Then he realized Macoran would have seen to a proper burial of the bones and ashes and his relief dissipated.

Stefan made his way back toward the wall where their weapons once hung. He leaned down and picked up his father's blackened three-pronged spear minus the long wooden handle.

"What does a Limond want on our land?"

Stefan dropped the spear, spun around and put his hand on his sword. The man already had his sword drawn and it took a moment for Stefan to look from it to the Macoran's face, "William?"

"By God in Heaven, 'tis it truly ye, Stefan? We thought ye buried by now." William quickly shoved his sword back in his sheath.

Stefan stepped out of the ruins, walked to him and locked forearms with his old friend. He was afraid of the answer, but he had to ask, "Are they dead?"

"Nay, just moved. The cottage burned not long after ye went missing. Macoran insisted they live in the village and make belts. With ye gone, they could not make a go of the place anyway. I asked Macoran to let me have the land, but he feared Kannak and Jirvel would see it as a sign ye were not coming back." He slowly looked Stefan up and down. "Ye fell in the river I see. Ye are all wet."

Stefan's relief was so overwhelming he only half heard what William was saying. "Did Jirvel agree to live in the village?"

"The two o' them were so mournful, they dinna care where they lived. What happened to ye?"

"I was sold."

"What?"

"'Tis a long story. Have Jirvel and Kannak taken husbands?"

"Kannak waits for ye and Jirvel breathes fire when any man

suggests it. Macoran had the priest declare her husband dead last year…ye were sold?"

"Into slavery."

William's mouth dropped. Then he gathered his wits. "Come home with me. Andrina will be as happy to see ye and ye could use a good drying out." He noticed Stefan look toward the village and knew what he was thinking. "Ye'd not like her to see ye looking like a wet dog and in Limond colors. Come with me. I have an extra Macoran shirt."

*

William loaned Stefan a blanket to wrap around his waist while Andrina hung his clothing near the hearth to dry. If she noticed the scar on his back, she did not mention it. "Kannak will be so happy to see ye." Just then, a baby cried and she went to the other room to fetch it.

"A laddie or a lassie?" Stefan asked.

William beamed. "A laddie and I could not be more proud. I can help ye build a new cottage after the harvest. Blair and some o' the other lads will help as well."

"I am thinking o' starting my own clan."

William watched his wife come back out with the baby and exchanged a look with her. "I am tempted to go with ye."

"And leave this fine land?"

"'Tis fine land indeed, but there are times I feel we labor just to satisfy the tithe."

"There was a time," said Stefan, "when yer tithe kept us fed and the tithe from the weavers and the cobbler provided us with warm clothing and badly needed shoes that fit. The tithe be a good thing, but perhaps a little less would do."

"Then we would like to be in yer clan."

"Aye, but we have no tools, few horses, even fewer weapons and no cottages. 'Twill be a hard life in the beginning."

"Then we will think on it." William poured wine into a goblet and handed it to Stefan. "Blair has married again and Diarmad be betrothed. Both be fine young lasses."

"I am pleased to hear it on both counts. Is Macoran yet married?"

"Aye, Mistress Agnes be still among us though she be so sickly looking we dinna know what holds her up." William smiled at his wife's giggle and took the baby from her so she could join them at the table. "We named him Stefan."

Stefan's eyes lit up. "My father gave me the name after his grandfather."

William leaned just a little closer. "Tell the truth o' it, are ye the Viking we could not find after the attack?"

Stefan rolled his eyes. "Have they not caught him yet?"

He ate the noon meal with them, told of his months of slavery and tried to be patient while his clothing dried, but it was growing more difficult by the minute. At last he could stand it no more and stood up. "I must see her or I will go daft."

William laughed. "I dinna expect ye to make it this long. Dress and I will get the horses. Do ye still ride without a saddle?"

"I prefer it."

"So do I, not that we can manage to save enough for fine saddles, what with the tithe the way it is. We...," he was still talking after he walked out the door.

William's pants were too short for Stefan, so he opted to put his damp pants back on. He was almost finished lacing his shoes when Andrina came back inside and noticed the calluses on his knees. He stood up, kissed her lightly on the forehead, touched the baby's cheek and smiled. "'Tis only from hard work."

In two short days his life had changed from exhausting labor to freedom and riding a horse bareback felt good. He followed William out of the small courtyard and turned down the path toward the village. "What caused the cottage to burn?"

"We dinna know. Jirvel and Kannak were in the village when I first saw the smoke. I am not afraid to say my heart stopped. By the time I got to it, I could not have saved either o' them had they been inside. It burned quickly and very hot. Even the oak tree next to it burned."

"Did others come?"

"Aye, but by then all we could do was keep it from spreading."

"And ye dinna know how it started?"

"Nay. Jirvel vowed the fire in the hearth was put out afore they left. But then, an ember might have blown out on the floor. I've seen that happen a time or two when the wind blows hard enough."

Stefan changed the subject. "Have ye seen the black stallion?"

"The gift from God, Jirvel calls it? Nay, no one has seen him since he helped Kannak escape. She talks about it often, but then she talks about ye constantly."

"I think about her constantly too."

"Love…it will either kill us or cure us…o' what, I am not quite certain." William laughed and kicked the side of his horse. "Come on,

Stefan, yer love has waited long and hard."

They were almost around the bend when Stefan suddenly halted his horse. "William?"

William stopped, turned his horse around and went back. "What is it?"

"I must see Macoran alone afore I let anyone know I am alive." William started to protest, but Stefan put up a hand to stop him. "Go to Macoran and bring him back without his guard."

"What should I tell him?"

"I dinna know…tell him ye've a surprise for him only."

William hesitated, but the look on Stefan's face assured him it was serious, so he turned his horse and rode off.

Stefan guided the dapple gray into the trees and dismounted. He prayed his suspicions were wrong but feared they were not. If he was right, only Macoran would know who to trust and what to do.

It seemed like it was taking forever for William to come back and he ran his hand through his hair repeatedly. Finally, he heard horses, peeked around a tree, made sure it was William with Macoran and then stepped out.

Macoran slowed and cautiously approached the man wearing Limond colors, until at last he saw the face of the tall, muscular man wearing it. Instantly, his eyes lit up and he quickly got down off his horse. "Stefan? Ye are not dead? We had nearly given up hope."

"Nay, I am not dead but there be danger still. Come and I will explain it." He led them into the forest and waited until all three were standing close together. "My snatching was planned."

"What? By whom?" Macoran asked.

"Brodies."

Macoran spat on the ground. "Those blackguards! I'll see they…"

"Ye dinna know who it was?"

"Kannak was so frightened she could not remember the colors o' the lads who chased her. Ye were on Limond land and…"

"Limond be my grandfather."

Macoran was so shocked he had to lean against a tree for support. "Good heavens, that is bad news."

CHAPTER XVIII

Stefan was beginning to get frustrated. There was so much to tell and he wanted to see Kannak. At least William had stopped asking questions. "If ye will allow it, I will explain."

"Please. Should I sit down?" Macoran asked.

"If ye prefer, but I doubt ye would stay down for long. 'Twas yer wife who arranged my snatching." Macoran's mouth dropped and he started to speak, but Stefan wouldn't let him. "Toran was captured with me."

"Toran the thief? The one I flogged in the courtyard? He run off just a day or two afore."

"He did not run off, he was sent with a message to yer wife's father. Just afore Toran died, he told me everything. She sent him to say these words exact: 'My husband does not come to my bed. He shames me with another just as yer wife shamed ye. The proof be his daughter.'"

Macoran could hardly speak. "She wanted…she knew Kannak was my daughter and…" He suddenly realized William was there and turned to see the look of shock on his face. But William was smiling. "Ye knew?"

"Everyone knows; she looks just like ye and not at all like Eogan. The only one who dinna know be Kannak."

"Kannak knows too and has for…but that matters not. Stefan, are ye saying my wife hoped for war?"

"Aye, she wanted ye dead and she would have gotten her desire for they are a very large clan with many warriors."

"How well I know. So why are we talking here, hiding in the forest like thieves?"

"Because their plan did not work. Toran was with the Brodies that day and they intended to come up the river at night and take Jirvel and Kannak. For Jirvel and Kannak ye would have gone to war and even if ye did not die, at least Agnes could cause torment by ridding ye o' the lass and the daughter ye loved. Toran was then to come back to ye and say he saw Brodies take them. But they found us instead at the castle and Kannak got away."

"Go on, I am listening."

"I fear yer wife was so furious she tried to burn Jirvel and Kannak alive."

At that, Macoran looked for a place, spotted a log and had to sit down. "I knew the lass hated me, but …"

"Laird Brodie could not release me, so he sold Toran and me into slavery."

Macoran shook his head in disgust. "What say ye I do?"

"Mistress Macoran will be none too pleased to see me. Ye must make certain she has no opportunity of trying to harm Jirvel and Kannak again." It was enough, and Stefan could wait no more. "Where be Kannak?"

"Where she always be this time o' day. Atop the hill watching the ocean."

Stefan grinned, handed his horse's reins to William and started up the hill.

*

William watched Stefan go and then turned to Macoran. “What will ye do now?”

“I will marry the lass I have loved for years.”

“Aye, but afore that?”

“Afore that, I must set aside my wife and get her out of my clan.”

“Tis not easily done,” said William. He offered his hand and helped his laird stand up.

“Nay, or I would have done it afore now.” He shook his head in disbelief again. “Never had I guessed Agnes might attempt to have us all killed. A war would have…”

“Aye, but ye have no proof o’ that.”

“I have Stefan.”

“He only heard it from a man who be now dead and no one saw yer wife…or her sons start the fire. I doubt the priest will believe any o’ it.”

“Twas the twins who most likely set the fire.”

“Aye.”

“There must be a way to rid us o’ all three.”

William mounted his horse and waited for Macoran to do the same. “What does a priest always believe be just cause for setting a wife aside?”

“Adultery? But who would believe it? I had to get so drunk, I do not even recall doing it and I assure ye, it was only once.”

“Perhaps it was not ye?”

Macoran guided his horse out of the trees and turned up the path toward the village. “Aye, but the laddies look just like me.”

“Are ye blind? They look just like her. They are skinny malinky longlegs and their father could be any man with red hair. Besides, they are hateful, spiteful laddies just like their mother. The Macorans would be well rid of the three of them.”

“I dinna deny that. I tried to…do ye really think the priest would believe it?”

“Are ye willing to swear ye never bedded her?”

*

Kannak had her arms folded and was looking out across the ocean watching for Viking ships or sea monsters. She had not seen either since Stefan was taken, but she watched for them daily just the same. Her waist length auburn hair was unbound, not because she preferred it, but because she neglected to braid it before she left the cottage. Jirvel often commented that the color of her frock was nearly the same as her hair, and they both found it amusing.

She sometimes dreamed Stefan had found the Vikings and their longships would bring him home, but other times she thought it a silly dream. This day there were storm clouds to the north and a beautiful rainbow arching across the sky. She loved rainbows and it eased her heart a little.

Sometimes she could not remember what he looked like and it plagued her. Other times if she closed her eyes, she could still feel his arms around her. Today, even that didn’t help. At least she stopped crying when she came to watch the waves. All crying did was give her a headache and make her mother sad. But not crying did not mean the hurt in her heart had gone away. Others said in time her heart would heal, but they were wrong.

Kannak reached out and touched the last drop of dew on the leaf of a tree and without even realizing she was saying it out loud, she whispered, “Will we ever be happy, Stefan?”

In a whisper just as soft, he said, “Aye.”

She dared not turn around for fear her ears deceived her. It sounded like his voice, but she thought her mind was playing tricks. Her heart would surely break all over again if she turned and he was not there.

“I love ye.”

Still she was afraid to look. Then she felt him come closer and put his arms around her from behind, the way he did when she was looking out the window of the hidden castle. “It is truly ye?”

“Aye.” He felt her lean against him and closed his eyes. At last she was back in his arms.

“I have missed ye so.”

“I have missed ye too. We will be happy now, I pledge it.”

“Ye cannae promise happiness, no one can.”

“I can pledge to love ye until the day I die.”

Finally, she turned in his arms and pulled away enough to look at him. He had not changed much except he had grown a thicker beard and his hair was lighter than she remembered. He was the most handsome man she had ever seen and his blue eyes seemed more brilliant than ever before. Kannak lifted her hand and traced the side of his face with her fingertips. “Am I forgiven?”

“For what?”

“For tricking ye into going to the hidden castle. I have wished for that day back so very often."

He took a moment to brush a stand of hair away from her face. "Ye cannae have that day back, I forbid it. That was the day ye gave me a reason to live. As to the castle, I hope to make it our home after we are married."

"Live in the hidden castle?"

"Aye. Would ye like it if we did?" At sixteen she was even more beautiful than he remembered. He touched her long silky hair and felt her lay her head on his chest.

"I would like that very much." She was still a little afraid she was sleeping and would wake to find him gone. But he felt so real. "Where have ye been?"

"I have been with ye. I have loved ye and prayed for ye and sent ye all kinds o' messages in my mind. Did ye not receive them?"

She giggled, pulled away a little and looked up at him. "What messages?"

"Each night I told ye I was not dead and each morning I told ye to wait for me."

"Then I must have gotten them for I would not believe ye were dead…and I waited." She slipped her arms around him and laid her head back on his chest. "Dinna let go o' me, Stefan. Dinna ever let go o' me."

"I will never let go." At last, she lifted her head and he lowered his lips to hers.

*

The priest sat at one end of the table and Macoran sat at the other. Between them were Agnes Macoran and her two twelve-year-old sons, one on each side of her. Seated across from her, William waited patiently.

The priest finished writing something down and then looked up. "And why has it taken ye all this time to bring it to my attention, Laird Macoran?"

Macoran was not prepared for that question and scratched his head trying to think of a reason.

"Because I just this morning confessed," said William. His words shocked him as much.as it did everyone else. Then he narrowed his eyes and pointed at Agnes, "She did it."

"Ye bedded her?" the astonished priest asked.

"Nay, 'twas my uncle."

It was the first Macoran heard anything about an uncle, but he was entranced with the story.

The priest frowned, "If that be the case, I will hear it from yer uncle."

William crossed himself and hung his head, "Dead these five years I am sad to say. I miss him still."

"Be silent," Agnes shouted. "Ye lie."

"I dinna lie, I saw it. Ye tempted him, ye did and I saw it."

"When?"

William found her question confusing. "Years ago, afore yer sons were born."

Agnes scooted her chair back and stood up. "Are ye saying these are not Macoran's sons?"

Finally getting his wits about him, Macoran spoke up. "They are not."

"They are not?" the priest asked. "How do ye know?"

He glanced at his wife and then turned his full attention to the priest, "I swear to ye that lass has never been in *my* bed."

Growing more incredulous by the moment, the priest's mouth dropped. "Not in all these years?"

"Truly, Father, would ye?"

The priest studied Agnes' feeble looks, realized he was staring at her too long and looked away. "And William, ye will swear it 'twas yer uncle?"

"I will," said William. He wondered for a moment just how much trouble he was going to be in with God, but the damage was done and it was too late. Besides, the crime Agnes plotted was far worse than his tiny little lie. When he looked, both of her sons were staring at her and she was backing away.

"My father will not take me back if I am accused o' adultery."

Macoran finally stood up. "Then ye have a problem, my dear, because I will not have ye either."

"What will I do, where can I go?"

It was something Macoran had not considered and he paused to think about it. "If ye will leave, and leave quickly, and if the priest agrees, what happened here today will not cross our lips. What ye tell yer father be up to ye." Inwardly he smiled. The twins would surely tell on her and she deserved punishment.

"And my sons?"

"Take them with ye. Should they ever grow up to be lads o' honor, I will welcome them back. But I suspect they will be far happier with the Brodies. Are we agreed?"

She had no choice. The priest was nearly finished writing on the parchment and all Macoran had to do was sign it. “Ye will send a guard with us?”

“Aye, I will send them until ye are across Limond land, after that…” he watched her dart up the stairs, heard her screech at her sons to gather their things and then slam the door to her bedchamber. Macoran went to the front door, opened it, yelled for his guard to make ready and came back to the table. He wanted desperately to smile, to laugh, to jump for joy. But he held his emotions until he made his mark on the parchment, thanked the priest and handed him a gold coin for his trouble.

It was another tedious hour before Agnes had her things situated, the horses loaded, and the boys in tow. Macoran stood on the landing, watched the three of them mount their horses and then nodded for his guard to take them away. He wanted to savor the moment and when Agnes glared back at him, he blew her a kiss.

*

Stefan and Kannak would have stayed on the hill top the rest of the day just holding each other, but there was some sort of commotion in the village. Both of them moved quickly to the place where they could see the shore. There were no longships.

Stefan laughed. “And to think I was a Viking once. Now I am afraid they will come back.” He took her hand and started down the path. “I cannae wait to see Jirvel.”

“Stefan, ye are dragging me again.”

“Oh.” He stopped, kissed her passionately and then slowed his pace. “Is she well?”

"She will be once she sees ye?" There were more shouts in the village and as they grew closer, they sounded more like a celebration than a battle.

Even Jirvel came out to see what all the commotion was. The people were dancing, shouting, clapping their hands loudly and she could make no sense of it. Before she could resist, Macoran suddenly grabbed her around the waist, kissed her breathless, lifted her up and carried her toward the courtyard.

"Put me down!"

"Not until we are married."

"Ye have gone daft, finally."

Macoran stopped and tried to kiss her again, but she refused. "Did I not say? Agnes has been set aside. Seems her sons are not mine."

Jirvel didn't believe him. "Put me down."

He did as she said, but he did not let go of her. "Marry me, Jirvel and make us both happy."

She realized everyone had abruptly gotten quiet and turned to see what the matter could be now. Just as they all were, she found herself staring at a Limond shirt. But when the man opened his arms to her, she finally recognized him and ran. "Stefan!"

Stefan wrapped his arms around her and began to swing her all the way around. Then he set her down and let her touch his face.

"I cannae believe it is truly ye. What a glorious day this be and I see ye have found Kannak. Good. I..." Tears came to her eyes and she hugged him again. "My son be home."

"And yer husband to be is waiting for an answer." Macoran folded his arms and began tapping his toe.

Jirvel turned to her daughter. “He claims he has set Agnes aside. Do ye believe him?”

“‘Tis the first I heard o’ it.”

William took up a position next to his laird, “I am witness to it myself. She be gone and gone for good.”

Conspiratorially, Jirvel leaned closer to her daughter. “Him I believe. Should I marry Macoran?”

“Aye,” said Kannak, “but this time we should lock him away so he has no opportunity of changing his mind on yer wedding day.”

Every eye was on them and everyone seemed to be leaning closer to hear what they were saying. Stefan put one arm around each woman. “Do the Marocans yet have a priest?”

“Aye,” both answered at the same time.

“Then I suggest we find him and get married today afore anything can go wrong.”

Kannak leaned around Stefan and looked at her mother. “I think he means all four o’ us.”

“I think he does too.”

Macoran cleared his throat. “Make up yer mind, lass. I have waited long enough to call ye mine. Say it afore the priest gets away.”

“Aye!” Jirvel shouted. She ran back to him, threw her arms around his neck and kissed *his* breath away. When they realized the crowd was cheering, both of them blushed.

*

For having no time to prepare, the weddings were a grand affair. Several of the women gathered flowers and made wreaths for Jirvel and Kannak’s hair. As soon as they were changed into their better clothing and their hair was brushed, they donned the wreaths and came back to the courtyard where the priest, Stefan and Macoran waited. And just before he began, Macoran slipped another two coins in the priest's hand in hopes of a shortened ceremony. It did not matter, of course, the four of them were so blissfully happy they hardly heard the words anyway.

Their wedding feast was as tasty as the clan could manage on such short notice and served to the couples at the long table in Jirvel's new home. The singers came to sing, the flutist played a happy jig and when the feast was over and all of the others were gone, Macoran closed the door and the great hall finally got quiet.

Stefan kissed his wife and then stood up. He walked to Macoran's trophy wall, lovingly touched his father's shield and then took it down off the wall. Once too large for him to manage, he slipped his hand through the grip in the back and it fit perfectly. He had grown up and was no doubt every bit as big as the great commander of so many Viking ships.

"'Tis yer's if ye wish to have it," Macoran said behind him. "Was it yer father's?"

Both Jirvel and Kannak were shocked. "Ye knew?" they both asked at the same time.

Macoran rolled his eyes. "Did ye truly think ye could hide a Viking among us without my knowing?"

"Does everyone know?" asked Kannak.

"If not, they are daft. My guards did not see a lad his size pass onto our land from the north or from any other direction. But he was just a laddie so we let it pass."

Jirvel had not taken her eyes off of Stefan. "Be it yer father's shield, Stefan?"

"Aye."

"Then it belongs to ye," said Macoran.

Stefan turned around and grinned at Macoran. "'Tis not enough. I will have Anundi's sword as well."

"This sword…with the golden handle? I love this sword."

"So did Anundi."

"Who be he?"

"He was my father's second but now has taken his place as commander and I will have his sword."

Macoran took a deep breath and looked to Jirvel for help, but she was not forthcoming. "I suppose," he began, "if ye were to promise to bring my daughter to see us often, I might…be persuaded. Though I love this sword. It fits my hand perfectly. Jirvel, do something, he be yer son."

Jirvel stood up, walked to her husband and took his hand. "What I have in mind dinna have to do with *our* son." She led him toward the stairs. "Which bedchamber be ours?"

Stefan laughed, watched them go, hung his father's shield back up and held out his hand to his wife. "Have we a place to sleep?"

"Now we do, now that mother lives here. Come, I will show ye." She kissed him passionately and then took him home.

*

Every clan had a beginning, and so it was that this small clan began in a hidden castle. The Viking named the clan after Jirvel's brother, Greagor, and they called themselves MacGreagors. One by one, the men who served as slaves with Stefan brought their families and friends, and by spring the clan numbered sixty-seven. They built stone cottages, for if they knew anything at all, they knew how to build.

Stefan used his father's money to buy the tools, seed, horses and weapons needed, beyond those the other men brought, and his grandfather sent as wedding gifts. He named William his second in command and soon, Diarmad and Blair together with their families, joined them. Naturally, they made an alliance with the Macorans and all lived in peace, even with the Brodies – although the Brodies were far from easily trusted.

He took Kannak often to see her parents and the two elders came often to swim in the warm water of the loch. But Macoran would not part with Anundi's sword and it became a running joke between them. After all, Stefan was to save ten women and he had yet to save any after Jirvel.

His grandfather came often too. He hired a new builder and this time he paid men to reinforce his castle. Their strained relationship turned more pleasant as the days went by and both learned how to laugh again. Stefan often thought about the day they landed and wondered if his father meant to land them on Limond land instead of Macoran. If so, it was a mistake Stefan thanked God for every day.

At least he learned to listen to his foreboding and not wait to take action. He thought he saw the gray wolf once, but it did not stay and the black stallion never did come back. He found that comforting, for it must mean Kannak was safe…at least for now.

But Laird Stefan Macgregor had a thing on his mind he could not dismiss. So one evening, he gathered his clan and proclaimed an edict.

For all the women he said, “Heretofore, no lass will be betrothed to a lad she dinna want.”

For his father and his grandmother’s sake, he said, “Heretofore, any lad who forces a lass shall be put to death.”

And for Jirvel and Kannak, he said, “Heretofore, any lad who lays hand on a lass, a laddie or a lassie out of anger, or drunkenness, or spite, shall also be put to death.”

Therefore, the edict was handed down to all the sons Kannak gave her husband, and from them, it continued to pass from generation to generation.

~ the end ~

MORE MARTI TALBOTT BOOKS

The Viking Series

Marti Talbott's Highlander Series

Marblestone Mansion, (Scandalous Duchess Series)

Lost MacGreagor Stories

Seattle Quake 9.2

The Carson Series

The Promise, Book 1

Broken Pledge, Book 2

Leanna A short story

M. T. Romances

Missing Heiress, Book 1

Greed and a Mistress, book 2

The Dead Letters, book 3

The Locked Room, book 4

Love and Suspicion, book 5

Keep informed about new book releases and talk to Marti on Facebook at: facebook/marti talbott

Sign up to be notified when new books are published at:

www.martitalbott.com

23555003R00123

Printed in Great Britain
by Amazon